Rachel's Road to Love

Great Smoky Mountain Getaways

Elsie Davis

Sweet Romance Publishing

@2021 Elsie Davis

All rights reserved. Except as permitted under the U.S. Copyright Act of 1976, no part of this publication may be reproduced, distributed or transmitted in any form or by any means, or stored in a database or retrieval system without the prior written permission of the publisher.

Cover Design by getcovers.com

Edited by Elaine Hyatt (Clarity Editing Services) & Cassandra Cornell

This is a work of fiction. Names, characters, organizations, places, events, and incidents are either products of the author's imagination or are used fictitiously. Any resemblance to actual persons, living or dead, or actual events is purely coincidental.

Sweet Romance Publishing

Sweetromancepublishing.com

PO Box 778

Liberty, NC 27298

Hebrews 11:1

"Faith is the reality of what we hope for, the proof of
what we don't see."

Chapter One

❤

THE BIGGEST DAY OF her life, and Rachel was as nervous as a mouse cornered by a cat. She had always pictured her wedding day as one filled with laughter and excitement, with the bride the center of attention as she walked down the church aisle on her father's arm. And with Leslie, her best friend since forever, helping her to get dressed, do her makeup, and calm her nerves.

Instead, she was alone in the dressing room, gazing at her reflection in the mirror and not liking what she saw. She turned away, wishing Leslie would return soon. Her friend had received a text and practically flown out of the room mumbling something about wedding details. That was at least thirty minutes ago. Besides, wasn't that what they hired a wedding planner for?

Rachel paced the room, adjusting and readjusting the dress, which seemed far too loose, sagging in all the wrong places. Stopping in front of the mirror, she stared back at her reflection, not recognizing the person standing there. The makeup was too much, the dress overly frou-frouy with puffed sleeves. The tiara and veil were dripping with tiny pearls that looked more like raindrops. No stranger to a camera, she knew it would look like she had splattered her face with cake batter in the wedding photos. The long train was fit for a regal princess, but then, her mother had insisted that it was precisely the right look for her daughter. Even her hair cascaded in long, tight ringlets down the side of her face, adding to the pomp and circumstance of the entire event.

None of which Rachel would have picked for herself.

Unfortunately, she had left the wedding planning to her fiancé, hoping Alex, her mother, her soon-to-be mother-in-law, and the wedding planner could handle everything. At the time, pawning off the wedding details had seemed like an excellent idea. It allowed her to do what she loved—serve others by sharing the word of God and helping to educate children in remote areas of the world. Not to mention, the decision had allowed Rachel to honor her commitment to join the South America mission trip team.

But over the past week since her return, Rachel wasn't so sure. From her appearance to the grandiose church wedding, flowers, and banquet reception to be held afterward, it was an over-the-top spectacle of an event. And nothing like she had envisioned in her head. Small, quiet, and full of awe and joy, a wedding focused on love, not some show to be captured in photos and splashed across bridal magazines.

Rachel glanced at the clock. Fifteen minutes until the wedding started. Where was her father? And where was Leslie? She moved to the window and stared out at the parking lot overrun with vehicles. Tiny snowflakes fluttered to the ground, leaving the barest trace of snow. Luckily, the storm was still hours away. By then, she'd be on her way to the airport and sunshine on her honeymoon.

A few last-minute guests pulled in, parked, and hurried inside the church. Everyone had come to see the matrimonial union of Alex Chesterfield and Miss

Rachel Harrelson, son and daughter of two of the most prominent families in Edgewood. In the county, for that matter.

The timing of Alex's proposal had been way wrong, and the well-rehearsed public setting had prevented her from saying no. Not that she wouldn't marry him— as it had always been the plan. However, the parents had been pushing them to take the next step in their relationship. At the time, neither they nor Alex had known about the mission trip in South America she'd signed up for and eagerly accepted. Unwilling to cancel out and leave the team hanging, she accepted the ring but made sure Alex knew she'd be gone a year. Her fiancé hadn't minded in the slightest, proof they were well suited.

So why was she so nervous? Her mother called it bride jitters, claiming they were expected. Rachel glanced at the clock on the wall again. Five minutes until the wedding started, and there was still no sign of her father or Leslie. Rachel took a deep breath, hoping to calm the dratted butterflies in her stomach.

The door opened, and her father walked in. "You look beautiful, sweetheart. The most beautiful bride I've ever seen."

"Thanks, Daddy. I could put a bag over my head, and you'd still tell me I look good." Rachel smiled, knowing it was true. Her father had always been there for her, helping Rachel maneuver through the twists and turns of life and keeping her controlling mother, well, somewhat under control.

"That may be true, but there's no need to stretch the truth. Alex will fall in love with you all over again when he lays eyes on you." Her father's warm smile did wonders to make her feel better.

Alex loved her. That is what she needed to focus on, not the fear she secretly harbored that this was a mistake. She loved Alex. They had been friends for a long time before they dated, and after years of dating, this was the natural next step. It's what everyone expected.

"Then let's do this," Rachel said, taking her father's arm as he held it out to her.

The door burst open, and Leslie came rushing into the room. But, unfortunately, her maid of honor was anything but the calm, cool, collected friend Rachel needed by her side.

"We've got a problem," Leslie said, her voice tight with tension.

"Let me guess, my mom's not happy with the flowers? Or is it the view from the front row pew?" Rachel teased, knowing her mother could be demanding. It was supposed to be the maid of honor calming down the bride, not the other way around.

"I wish. Don't get me wrong, your mother is having a hysterical meltdown, but it's not for either of those reasons. Honestly, I wish it were," Leslie said, shaking her head and reaching for Rachel's hand. "Honey, I'm so sorry." Her friend's eyes pooled with tears, the thin-set line of her lips in direct contrast.

Something was seriously wrong. "Has something happened to Alex? Was he in an accident? Tell me," Rachel pleaded.

"He's going to wish he had been in one when I get through with him," Leslie ground out. "He's not coming today—or any other day for that matter. Roger was shocked when he got a call from Alex and was told to call off the wedding. Apparently, even his best man didn't know Alex had misgivings. I could kill Alex for doing this to you," Leslie said, her voice rife with anger.

The room started to spin. This couldn't possibly be happening to her. Rachel grabbed onto a nearby chair for support. "What?" she squeaked out.

In all the times she'd thought about her wedding day, never once had the vision included being left at the altar.

Jilted.

Rachel felt faint and crossed the room to sit on the sofa, rubbing her temples with her fingertips to ease the headache that was forming. She ripped off the veil, trying to make sense of what Leslie was telling her and the implication of her runaway groom.

"He doesn't want to get married. I can't imagine why he waited until the last minute to figure this out and tell you. Alex is a mouse, not a man, and he doesn't deserve you."

"Where is he now?" her father asked, his face red with fury. "I need to have a chat with that boy. This is unacceptable. No one stands my daughter up and gets away with it. I thought he was better than this."

"Daddy, let it go. Please, it won't change anything. Maybe Alex has a case of cold feet, and this is just bad timing." Rachel had her own jittery nerves to deal with—she just hadn't been brave enough to call off the wedding and figure out why.

"Cold feet? Let's hope so. Of all the rotten things he could do to you. And on your wedding day. Not to mention there's a lot of money tied up in this event." Her father's practical side was showing. Rachel wouldn't put it past him to demand the Chesterfield family reimburse him since Alex pulled a disappearing act.

"I know, and I'm sorry." Rachel fought to hold herself together and not give in to the urge to fall apart. She took several deep breaths, trying to quell the rising agitation threatening to explode.

Leslie sat next to her. "Everyone's downstairs, waiting to see you. They feel awful. Even Alex's family has stayed. They are equally furious with him," she said, rubbing Rachel's back with soothing strokes.

"I don't want to talk to anyone. What would I say? Please, make them go away, Daddy." She looked up at her father, imploring him to take over the situation. Just like he always did when things got out of hand.

"I'm on it, sweetheart. I should see to your mother anyway, as I'm sure Leslie's description of your mother's hysterical meltdown was an understatement of her condition."

Rachel knew she could trust her father to manage everything. When the door closed, she turned to Leslie. "What am I going to do? Even if Daddy gets rid of them now, they will still come to see me and want answers I can't give. And think of the wedding gifts that need to be returned. It's just too much, right now." Rachel rocked back and forth, hugging herself, trying to stop the overwhelming sensation of nausea that threatened to take control.

"Let me think." Leslie stood and paced the room. "Why not go on your honeymoon alone? You could sneak out the back door. I drove your car here since mine was blocked in at your place."

Rachel shook her head. "No way. That would be awkward staying in a honeymoon suite for one. Think of all the pitiful looks I'd get then."

Leslie stopped pacing and turned to her. "I've got it. Go up to my family's cabin in the Smoky Mountains. It's only an hour from here, right close to the North Carolina border. Totally private."

Rachel had forgotten about the cabin Leslie and her brother inherited when their uncle died a couple of years ago. She and Leslie had talked about going up. Still, it never seemed the right time for them to coordinate clearing their schedules, especially with college workloads and then after that, she left on the mission trip. "I don't know. I'm not sure that's a good idea either. What about your brother? He might not like me staying there."

"He's still in Afghanistan on deployment. So you'd be doing me a favor by checking on the place. I promised Chad I would keep an eye on it, and I haven't been up there in weeks. There's a caretaker who looks in on the place occasionally, but other-wise, the responsibility has been mine."

Becoming a recluse, even if only for a short time, sounded ideal. Rachel was tempted. "Are you sure? And what about the storm that's headed this way? It's supposed to be a doozy."

Leslie frowned. "Stop looking for excuses not to go and look for reasons to say yes. It's the perfect answer to your dilemma. Stay as long as you like. Let me check the weather. The last I heard, it's still hours away." Leslie pulled out her phone, pushing a few buttons.

"There see." She held up her phone for Rachel to see the screen. "If you leave now, you'll be way ahead of the snowstorm and be hunkered down by a nice fire by the time it hits. It's a winter wonderland up there this time of year, and the cabin is already stocked with food basics. I'm sure you can make do. Although, you might want to stop for milk as I'm not sure powdered milk is your thing."

Her friend made it sound easy, and it did sound nice. And private. After a year on a mission trip, she'd learned to face challenges head-on, and this wasn't as complicated. She could handle a quick stop at a gas station for milk.

Leslie was right. The cabin would be ideal for what Rachel needed. Out of the limelight and away from people. People who would be all too willing to cast diplomacy out the window in exchange for the inside scoop on why Alex walked away.

Something Rachel wished she had an answer to as well. "Fine. I'll do it. And on the way, I'm going to call Alex and find out precisely what just happened and why."

"That a girl. I'll jot down the instructions. Just keep in touch with me. Oh, and I'll add the code for you to unlock the front door." Leslie snagged her purse off the dresser and took out a set of keys, and a paper and pen, jotting down some notes.

This whole scene was surreal. How many romance movies had she watched on Hallmark or the Up Family and Faith channel where someone was left at the altar? This was made for TV drama—not real life. "Thank you. I can't believe this is happening to me. Correction, happened to me."

Leslie hugged her. "Here are the keys to your car, the directions to the cabin, and the code to get it. Now get going before your mother appears, and you can't make an escape."

Rachel nodded. "You're right. And thank you for everything."

"That's what besties are for." Leslie peeked out the door and motioned for her to follow. It was all very secretive, adding to the already intense drama as Rachel made her escape.

They headed out the back door into the cold, blustery day. Rachel shivered with only her wedding dress to ward off the cold.

"Here, take my coat," Leslie said, reaching into the car to retrieve it from the back seat and helping Rachel put it on. "Lucky for you I left it here. Now get in and I'll be right back with your suitcase." Her friend pulled open the door and Rachel tried to slide in the driver's seat, a move made impossible by the sheer volume of material from the train of her gown.

"Wait. I know how to fix this little problem." Rachel yanked at the train, ripping the gown with an intensity that echoed her mood. Finally, the material gave way, and she handed Leslie the shredded remains. She started the engine and flipped on the heat. "Thanks, Leslie—for everything."

"You're welcome. Now let me get your suitcase from the limo driver. Wait here a minute, and I'll be right back." Leslie shut the door and made her way to the limousine that sat in front of the church.

After a brief discussion with the driver, the man popped open the trunk and pulled out her suitcase. Bless Leslie and her ever-efficient brain in a time of crisis. Returning to Rachel's car, she hoisted the bag into the back seat. "Not sure what you can use in here, considering you were bound for Rio. Lucky for you, we're about the same size, and I've got clothes at the cabin you are welcome to wear that should be more suitable."

Total understatement. Anything would be more suitable than the lingerie she'd bought for her wedding night. But, thinking about the nightie and what it signified made Rachel uncomfortable, the same way she felt when Leslie insisted she buy it in the first place.

Rachel nodded, putting the car in drive. Only once did she glance in the rearview mirror, checking out the church as it grew smaller. This morning started out as a wedding day, and now, it was nothing short of a disaster.

The problem was, Rachel wasn't so sure the disaster wasn't a blessing.

Chapter Two

♥

AFTER TYPING IN THE cabin's address on her navigation system, Rachel set the car on cruise control as she headed for the mountains. She wouldn't be able to use it on Black Mountain's steep grade, but while she could, she would.

Tugging out the bobby pins that held her curls in place, Rachel tossed them in the cupholder. It would have been better to ditch the dress, but nothing could be done about it until she reached the cabin. On the positive side of things, at least her gas tank was full, and she wouldn't have to stop along the way. Facing the curious gazes of people at a gas station as they took in her torn wedding gown was not high on her priority list. It was also the reason she decided to nix the idea of stopping for bread and milk. There was always tomorrow.

Snow flurries fell softly, the darkened skies more ominous than when she'd started out. It would seem the weatherman's prediction was slightly off, and the edge of the storm wasn't far behind her. With any luck, Rachel could keep it that way.

She scanned her fingerprint to unlock her phone. "Call, Alex," she said, activating her voice-controlled dial feature. The way he had gone about destroying their wedding day with a phone call to his best man was cold and heartless. No matter his reasoning, it hadn't been fair. In fact, it was downright weaselly and something totally unexpected from Alex.

"Hey, Rachel. Before you say anything, let me say I'm sorry. I know I was a jerk and that you didn't deserve this."

Darn straight, I didn't. "Well, you can start by telling me what the heck is going on? I was blindsided by this. If you were having second thoughts, why didn't you say anything before today? Before I had my dress on and my hair and makeup done. And before everyone was sitting in the church wondering where you were." Rachel was on a roll, and it all came rushing out. She hadn't planned what to say, not truly expecting him to answer the phone.

"It was cowardly, I know. But my parents...they were the ones who wanted this marriage, more than we did, I think. I'm sure he will cut me off financially because of this, but I just couldn't go through with the wedding. It wouldn't have been fair to you or me."

"But why? What changed?" she asked, trying to make some sense of her feelings about today's events.

"Let me ask you this. You went away for a year after we got engaged. Why? Why didn't you cancel the mission trip and stick around and plan the wedding with me? It was a life we were going to share together, and yet, you chose to have nothing to do with the planning and high-tailed it out of Edgewood."

Alex was right, and it was the same question she had been asking herself. "I don't know. You took me by surprise, and it wasn't like I could say no, not with everyone looking on and waiting for me to say yes. I was excited about the mission trip and the chance to help others, especially the children, and I couldn't say no to that either. The engagement was just bad timing. I figured the only way to make both parts of my life work was to let you all plan the wedding, while I went on the mission trip."

"What bride doesn't want to plan her wedding? Also, did you hear what you just said? '*It wasn't like I could say no.*' That sounds to me like you weren't sure even then."

Rachel hadn't been sure, and there lay the crux of the problem. "It was the right thing to do. You and I both know our parents had our wedding in mind for years, and we were just moving forward with the next logical step in our relationship." She winced, the words sounding awful even to her own ears. Logical and marriage were on the opposite side of the spectrum when it came to love.

"The right thing to do isn't a declaration of love," Alex insisted.

"Maybe not the way a married couple would be, but I figured we would grow into that part." Love was something that grew over time. Respect and trust were far more valuable traits. Although, it would seem Alex had wiped those traits away in one fell swoop.

"And there's the bottom line in all of this. You're my best friend, but I don't love you like a husband should love his wife. Tell me something. Were you upset when you found out I wasn't coming to the church, or did you feel a sense of relief?"

The truth was staring her right in the face. Rachel had been both relieved and upset, but in all honestly, the rush of relief had come first. The jitters weren't jitters at all. They were the fear she was making the biggest mistake in her life. "I don't know," she said, evading his question. "What changed your mind?"

"Honestly, Rachel, I'm not sure you want to know," Alex said, uncertainty lacing his voice enough to pique her interest further.

"Try me. We've come this far, and I'm not sure anything else can compare to being left at the altar."

"I fell in love with Brittany Adams. That's how I knew what you and I shared wasn't enough to sustain a marriage. I'm sorry."

Love? Alex was in love with someone else. She was wrong—this was just as bad. He'd ditched her for a new relationship with someone else. "Do I know...wait...are you talking about the wedding planner?"

"Yes. I swear it just happened. We spent so much time together planning the wedding, and we clicked.

Enough that I know it's real. I've never felt like this about someone before."

"Your timing stinks, Alex."

"I know, please forgive me. You know I never wanted to hurt you. We let the parents control far too many of our decisions—but not anymore. At least, not for me. But please, don't breathe a word of this to anyone. I want to keep my relationship with Brittany off the radar until things cool down. If my parents find out, they will never accept her into the family when it becomes known. So any chance at happiness and not being cut out of the family requires discretion at this point."

Rachel shook her head, still processing the newest information and how she felt about it. Not that it mattered. What was done was done. "So, why tell me?"

"I figure you deserved the truth. And I'm hoping as a friend, you will help me out."

They were friends. Rachel just needed time to get used to the sudden changes in her life. "Thank you for that. And since you told me the truth, I figure you deserve the same." She took a deep breath. "You asked me if I was relieved or upset when you were a no-show. The answer is I was relieved. Angry for sure, but those feelings came after a strange sense of relief." There was no way she could be mad at Alex for doing the right thing and saving them both from making a huge mistake.

"That makes me feel better about the whole thing. Not that I deserve to, but I hope you know what I mean," Alex said, a ring of sincerity in his voice.

"I do know what you mean."

"I also hope you will forgive me someday. There was no way I could go through with the wedding, knowing I was in love with someone else, and knowing that in the eyes of God, you and I were getting married for all the wrong reasons."

"I understand, and I've already forgiven you. Not your timing, but for stopping the wedding," Rachel admitted.

"I hope you find true love one day, Rachel. Then you'll be thanking me for ruining today."

"That won't be for a long time, trust me. In fact, I'm headed up to Leslie's family cabin for a few days, and I'm going to put in for more mission trips. I want to travel the world, and you've given me the freedom to do just that. Thank you." It felt as though a weight had been lifted from her shoulders.

"Take care, Rachel. Don't be a stranger as we are still friends, I hope."

"Yes, friends. You take care too." She might hate the way Alex handled the situation, but she was grateful he'd done what he did.

Her motto had always been to try and find the positives, even in the bad. And it was never more true than now. God must have known her heart, and now there was so much to be joyful for. Nothing was stopping her from making more mission trips, and all without her mother's interference. *Thank you, Lord.*

The snow had picked up in intensity while she was on the call, enough that it was sticking to the ground. She peered in front of her, not wanting to miss the next direction turn highlighted on her GPS.

Rachel turned onto the back road and flipped on her wipers, trying to keep the windshield clear of snow buildup. A weather alert flashed across her screen, the beeping sound ominous. She glanced at the phone to find out what was going on and clicked on the flashing winter storm warning. She couldn't read and drive, so she pulled into a small, run-down country store parking lot to stop. Tapping on a few keys, she brought up the radar, unsure of where she was and finding it easy to let her GPS locator figure it out.

Heavy blues, pinks, and purples filled the screen, moving across the black dot. The storm was now right on top of her, but there was no turning back. Just when she thought the day couldn't get any worse, Mother Nature was proving her wrong. Back on the road, Rachel followed the directions as they flashed on the screen, the trip was slow going as the snow increased to an almost blizzard-like intensity.

The salty mixture the road crews must have sprayed in advance of the storm was now turning the precipitation to mush. The area already had plenty of snow, but it was about to get a fresh dump of the white stuff.

Rachel glanced at the GPS screen, noting she only had ten miles to go. Unfortunately, every minute that passed became more treacherous. She was grateful when she made the final turn up the long driveway to the house. It was a steep incline, and her tires started to slip in the snow. Without salt or traffic, the snow was much deeper. She shifted the car into the anti-skid mode, hoping for more traction.

Half a mile more and she was home free according to the GPS. The car went into a slide toward the edge of the road. Rachel took her foot off the brake, gently trying to correct her direction, aiming more for the center of the driveway. Her wheels didn't respond, and she slid into the ditch, the car coming to a sudden stop as it rammed into a sign.

"*Arghhh!*" Rachel smacked the steering wheel, frustrated with the newest turn of events. She shifted into reverse, hoping to back the car out, but the tires just spun. The car was stuck, which left Rachel only one choice. *Walking.*

Rachel twisted around and grabbed her suitcase, pulling it into the front passenger seat. She kicked off her high heels and pulled on a pair of sneakers. She slid out of the car, the cold seeping through to her skin in record time.

Trudging up the road, one slippery step at a time, she was relieved when she spotted the cabin as she rounded a bend in the road. Her relief faded all too quickly as she noticed smoke billowing from the chimney. The warmth would have been a toasty welcome if it weren't for a tiny problem—there wasn't supposed to be anyone at the cabin.

What if someone had broken in and was using the place in the absence of the owners? Rachel had no choice but to go inside and look around, but it was of significant concern. Her friend had mentioned a caretaker, and that's precisely the scenario Rachel was hoping for. She called Leslie, hoping for answers but at the very least to have someone on the phone when she entered the cabin. Except Leslie's phone went straight to voice mail. No help there. And her parents were out of the question. They didn't know Rachel had come up here, and she wasn't ready to tell them.

Rachel entered the code and went inside, shivering uncontrollably—the satin wedding dress no match for the chill factor even with Leslie's coat. "Hello? Anyone here?" she called out, leaving her suitcase by the front door, and heading straight for the fireplace and heat. Five minutes later, her fingers and toes, and body were all sufficiently warmed against the roaring fire, and so far, no one had appeared.

She headed down the hall to investigate the small cabin and figure out what was going on. Maybe it was a simple matter of Leslie calling someone to open up the place in preparation for her arrival, and she was letting herself get carried away. The answer made perfect sense and would be just like something her friend would do.

At least it did until she spotted the duffle bag in the corner of the bedroom, as well as the toiletries laid out on the bathroom sink. No reassurance there that her reasonable explanation was still valid. Neither did the scent of Irish Spring that permeated the bathroom air. *Nothing old about the fragrance.*

Noises coming from the direction of the front room had Rachel on alert. She glanced around, spotting a baseball bat leaned up against the side of the dresser. Grabbing it, she headed down the hall, ready to face whatever, or whoever, she found. Adrenaline raced through her body, her heart pounding as she slowly eased toward the sounds.

A tall and decidedly handsome man looked up at her arrival. "What the—"

"Who are you?" Rachel stood her ground, bat in the air.

"Put that down. And tell me who you are and what you're doing here? This is my cabin," the man said, his scowl backing up his declaration.

Except, Rachel knew better. "You must be mistaken. This belongs to the McCarthy's. Leslie and Chad McCarthy, to be exact." She lifted her chin, defying the man to tell her otherwise.

"Like I said, lady. My cabin. I'm Chad McCarthy. I'm asking again, who are you?" He took a step closer.

Rachel stepped back. "Chad?" she repeated her voice more like a squeak. It didn't make any sense he would be here. Leslie had assured her he was still in Afghanistan.

"Yes. And for the fourth time, you are…"

"Rachel Harrelson. Leslie's best friend."

The guy seemed to relax considerably, but he might not be so happy about the situation when he realized her car was stuck in the ditch. "Okay, now we are getting somewhere. She's talked a lot about you over the years, but I don't believe we've ever had the pleasure of meeting."

He was wrong. They had met—once. The night she and Leslie had gone to their junior prom. Ten years older, the handsome man hadn't paid her one iota of interest. But, for Rachel, it had been a bit different. More like a case of adolescent love, at least, it had been until Alex asked her to go steady. "What are you doing here?" she asked, trying to make sense of his presence.

"I snowshoed up to Eagle Point, wanting to enjoy the view as the storm rolled in. What about you?" His gaze slid down her body and back up. "It's not as though I was expecting company, especially someone, *ummm*, who looks like a runaway bride."

"Wrong story."

"Excuse me," he asked, the lines across his forehead deepening.

"More like a jilted bride, so you're not far off." Laughing at herself would go a long way to helping her get through yet another unexpected twist to the day.

"I see. It was the sneakers that had me thinking otherwise," Chad teased, his smile softening his features.

Rachel grinned. *Runaway Bride* was one of her favorite romantic comedies. "Leslie thought this would be a good place for me to hide out and avoid all the sympathetic and prying eyes back in Edgewood. And she assured me you were out of the country."

"I was, but now I'm not. Things happened, and I wanted some time to unwind before I let my sister know I was back in the area." Chad ran a hand through his hair as if trying to decide the best way to deal with a situation not of his choosing.

Rachel could help him on that score. "This won't do at all. I can't stay here with you, seeing as we're not married."

"Not that I wanted company, but out of curiosity, why is that a problem?" he asked.

"It wouldn't be proper." Rachel shrugged, crossing her arms in front of her as a way to do something. Anything to ease her nerves. She hadn't meant to sound like an old fuddy-duddy prude. "Maybe you could run me back into town."

"I see. But in case you haven't noticed, unless you've got a snowmobile, your ticket out of here expired. And I'm not a minister, so you're plumb out of luck getting married, even if you are dressed for the part. So you're stuck with me, sister." His cheeky grin was her undoing.

"The dress comment is hitting below the belt, and I don't see the humor in the situation." Now she really did sound old, but his comment hurt. Nothing about today had been her fault. Well, not really anyway. If she'd never said yes to Alex in the first place, today would have never happened.

"Sorry, I was just trying to lighten your intensity. It's not like we have a lot of choices. Where's your car anyway?"

"About a half of a mile down the driveway firmly planted in a ditch."

"Which is exactly where it will stay until after the storm passes and the roads clear and someone can come tow it out. I'm guessing you don't have a four-wheel-drive vehicle. Lucky for you, the caretaker dropped off some food supplies and batteries in case the power goes out. He won't be back to check on me until things clear up enough for him to have time to get back up here. He'll be busy with the road crews once the storm passes."

"Do you have the answer to everything?" she asked sharply, her frustration bubbling over.

"I try." Chad shrugged, moving to the fireplace to add more wood.

Rachel shook her head. "I need to call Leslie, so if you'll excuse me." She turned and headed down the hall.

"She'll vouch for me—I *am* her big brother," Chad called after her.

Rachel stopped and turned around, staring back at the man she once secretly crushed on. "Maybe that's what worries me."

Chad's smile disappeared. *The question was...why?*

Chapter Three

♥

RACHEL MADE HER WAY down the short hallway to the bedroom—the only bedroom based on the look of things. Chad was right about her not being able to leave, but he had another thing coming if he thought she would take the couch. This was supposed to have been her wedding night, and instead, it was her jilted bride's night...if there was such a thing. And if ever there was an opportunity for chivalry, this would be it.

She shoved her suitcase into the corner and plopped down on the queen-size bed. The fluffy down comforter felt soft and heavenly. This was better than a hotel bed any day of the week. Pulling out her phone, she pressed the speed-dial button for Leslie.

"I'm so glad you called. I was starting to worry, what with the storm and all," Leslie said in a rush.

"I'm fine. Mostly anyway. The weather turned ugly quicker than expected, making the drive long and tense. On top of that, my car wasn't cut out for the snowy roads. I managed to put it in the ditch about a half-mile from the cabin. I had to park and walk the rest of the way. Not fun, but at least I had sneakers. Otherwise, I would have never made it." *And her story wasn't even close to finished.*

"I'm so sorry. This was supposed to be relaxing for you, not add insult to injury from Alex's treachery. At least you're there now. There should be plenty of firewood. Unfortunately, the storm has turned into a doozy, stalling out over most of the Appalachian Mountains and stretching from Pennsylvania to Georgia."

"You've got to be kidding. I should have never come here," Rachel said, letting out a heavy sigh.

"Why not? Don't you like it?" Leslie sounded hurt.

Rachel rolled over on her back and stared up at the ceiling. "The cabin is perfect, with one exception—it came occupied."

"Occupied? I don't understand. Is it a squatter? Are you okay?" Leslie had gone into protective mode, and Rachel was positive her friend would have been in the car and on her way here if not for the storm.

"It's your brother," she said, trying to put her friend's worry to rest, knowing the bomb she'd let drop would have an entirely different reaction.

"That's not possible," Leslie exclaimed. "He's in Afghanistan."

"Nope, he's here. And now, I'm here and snowed in with him. What a disaster."

"I can't believe he didn't tell me he was coming home. I'm so sorry. But talk about an unseen benefit in an awful day for you."

"Silver lining?" Rachel didn't see it that way at all.

"You're not alone during this snowstorm. The projections are now calling for four to five feet instead of the three in the original forecast. Talk about a game-changer. I feel better knowing Chad's there. He's a good guy, even if he is my brother."

Leslie's comment made sense, but not everyone would see the positive aspect her friend did. "My mother won't agree. She will have a conniption fit if she finds out. Her angelic daughter is shacked up with a man—*oh my*." Rachel grinned. "Nothing could be further from the truth, but you know how she likes to exaggerate."

"Don't tell her then. It's not like anyone will know, and when the storm passes, you leave. It's quite simple." Leslie was the voice of reason she needed. No one needed to know, and her reputation would remain intact and her mother off her back for a few days. It all sounded pretty good when put that way.

Rachel would take a proactive approach and send her mother a text to let her know she had arrived safely, but nothing more. Not even where she was for the time being. It's not as if the situation that triggered her flight was of her choosing. "I thought you always told me he was a ladies' man?" she asked, going back to the reason for this conversation in the first place.

"Oh, he is, and I'll be sure to give him the sisterly warning. After I chew him out for not telling me he was home, that is. I wonder how long he's back for. It would be awesome to see him again. Does he look good? I mean, he's not there because he's injured or anything, right?" Leslie asked, worry echoing in her voice.

"Not that I can tell. I mean, it's not like we had much to say to each other." *Other than the fact he wouldn't marry her.* Turned down for marriage twice in one day. Few ladies could share that claim to fame. "What's he like? I mean, what can I expect?"

"He was a tormentor when I was a kid. The older brother who didn't want his kid sister hanging around sort of thing. I remember once when he fixed me dinner, and he tricked me, using mushy mashed cauliflower instead of potatoes as a vegetable."

It sounded healthy and delicious. "What's wrong with that?"

"I hated cauliflower, and he knew it," Leslie said in disgust.

"So what happened? Did you spit it out—at him?" Rachel chuckled. Her friend was a fireball, and she wouldn't have put it past Leslie.

"Nope. I ate it."

"You didn't know?" Rachel asked, confused by Leslie's admission.

"No. Truth is, I don't like cauliflower, but when it's smashed, and you add butter, salt, and pepper, it tastes pretty good."

"So your tormentor did you a favor." Rachel laughed. Innocent fun from her perspective. Chad may have been ten years older, but any brother had to be more exciting than no sisters or brothers. This is why Rachel vowed to have a large family one day.

"I guess, but it was mean-spirited."

"Well, if he tries to cook me potatoes, I'll be on guard for a switch," Rachel teased.

"Laugh now, but he likes practical jokes. Oh, and don't let him near any scissors. Once, he cut my hair because I accidentally broke his bike. And then there was the time he locked me out of the house because I ratted him out to my mom that he'd gone on a date and snuck in the house late. I was only eight. What did he expect?"

"Hopefully, he gave you a good haircut," Rachel continued to tease her friend, rather enjoying the stories. They made Chad seem more real and personal.

"I can't believe you're defending him. Don't say you weren't warned," Leslie said, joining in the fun of the moment.

"I consider myself warned. Hopefully, Chad's grown out of practical jokes." It sounded more like

Leslie was a handful as a child and that her brother's payback methods were harmless enough. But if she was going to be stuck here with him a few days, she'd be on her best behavior so as not to test the man.

"Did you get a chance to talk to Alex?" Leslie asked. "I haven't heard from the snake, and neither has Bobby."

"Actually, I did. It was the right decision for both of us, just super lousy timing."

"You're far too generous in your attitude toward Alex."

"The thing is, I know more about what prompted his decision. I've promised not to say anything yet, but I will tell you since you're my best friend. But you are equally sworn to secrecy." There wasn't anything she wouldn't tell Leslie, and the last thing Rachel wanted was for her friend to continue to hate Alex over this.

"Start talking. You know I can keep a secret."

It was true. "The thing is, Alex and the wedding planner fell in love."

"No way."

"Yes, way. They don't want people to know yet because he's hoping his parents will come around to accept her. He's worried if they suspect Brittany is the reason Alex didn't marry me today, that they'll cut him out of the family business and never accept her."

"I still can't believe it, and his timing stinks."

"You'll get no argument from me on that point."

"And when I see him, I intend to give him a piece of my mind," Leslie said, still in best-friend protective mode.

"Let it go, Leslie. It's all for good."

"*Hmmmph.* After you left, your parents and Alex's parents were deep in conversation, and they stopped talking every time I got near them." Leslie knew they were controlling and had every right to worry.

There was no telling what they would concoct to salvage the wedded bliss they had planned for their children. "None of them will be happy, but it can't be helped. They wanted this wedding more than Alex and me. And speaking of wedding, I need to change out of this dress."

"Okay. And Rachel, I'm sure everything will be okay. Honestly, Chad is a good guy with a big heart. He's always been very protective of me, and I'm sure he'll do the same for my best friend."

"Thanks. I'll keep you posted." Rachel hung up and crossed the room to grab her suitcase, hefting it onto the bed. Shorts, short-sleeve tops, and bathing suits—nothing of use while snowed in at the cabin. She made her way to the closet, hoping Leslie was right and that there would be a better selection of clothes her friend had left behind.

Bingo. Blue jeans and a flannel shirt. The perfect combination for warmth and comfort. Tossing them on the bed, she reached to unzip her gown. Sliding the zipper down the first two or three inches, she moved her hand to come from underneath her arm to pull it down the rest of the way.

Except it wouldn't budge. Rachel tugged at it repeatedly, but the zipper was stuck. Rachel tried from the top again, hoping to pull it back up or push it down further. Nothing happened.

She let out a deep sigh. "*Arghhh*. Why me, Lord?" This just wasn't her day. It was either stay in her dress the entire time she was here or resort to asking Chad for help. Didn't seem like much of a choice. Rachel pulled open the door and headed down the hall.

As she entered the living room, Chad laid his phone down on the coffee table and looked up at her, his expression unreadable.

"I need help," she said, coming straight to the point.

"And I need a new ear. Leslie just chewed mine off for not telling her I was in town."

"That's not my fault. You should have called your sister. And then none of this would have happened because I wouldn't have come here."

Chad shook his head, tension radiating from his tightly drawn brow. "So much for quiet time. She'll be here as soon as the snowstorm stops and the roads are passable." He let out a deep sigh. "What do you need help with?"

"This," she said, pointing to her dress. "The zipper is stuck."

Chad stood. "Turn around. I can imagine it's not overly comfortable, both the dress and the memory it represents."

It was a nice sentiment, not to mention proof he could be understanding. Rachel did as she was instructed and turned around.

He pulled and yanked at the zipper, but Chad wasn't having any better luck than she was. "You've got it caught on the lace and silk. So unless you're partial to the dress, the easiest way to get it off you—is to cut it off."

Rachel spun around. "Is this a joke to you? I heard about how you cut Leslie's hair. She was adamant not to put scissors in your hands, so why don't you tell me what you've really got in mind. She warned me you're a practical joker." She leveled him with a stern gaze, letting him know she wouldn't tolerate any tomfoolery.

"I didn't realize you would still be sentimental about the dress." Chad frowned. "I'd think you would want to burn it. Besides, the material is already torn beyond repair, and the bottom is wet and dirty. I was making light of what needs to happen if you want to get out of the dress."

She wasn't going to explain it to him. *Turning the other cheek was more like it.* The expression had been drilled into her while growing up, and it stood her in good stead now. She didn't want revenge on Alex, and she didn't want to ruin any chance he might have to find happiness. In fact, Rachel was a little jealous he'd found someone to love, the marriage kind of everlasting love if he was to be believed. "Cut it off then." She turned around, wanting nothing more than to get this over with.

"Just so you know, I cut Leslie's hair because she painted my bike pink. It was the bike I used to get to work. I didn't go to work that day, and I lost my job at the grocery store. So I'd say it was a fair trade."

Rachel grinned. "Pink, huh? She left that part out."

Chad continued to work at the zipper in silence. The sound of fabric tearing made her cringe. It's not like she wanted the dress, and it was already ruined by the missing train and the walk in the snow, but she paralleled it to the closure of a chapter in her life.

"Got it," Chad exclaimed as the zipper broke free. "I, umm, err, think you should be good now," he said, stepping away and holding up his hands.

Realizing half her back was exposed, including her bra strap, Rachel felt her face grow warm. She took off down the hall to the privacy of the bedroom. Donning the jeans and flannel shirt, she felt much better. More relaxed.

Enough to get up the courage to face Chad again.

Rachel joined Chad in the kitchen, the smell of something cooking causing her stomach to growl.

He looked up as she approached. "I heated some hearty clam chowder for dinner, and we've got oyster crackers and sourdough bread. Figured you would be hungry."

"It sounds good. Why are you acting so nice?" Rachel asked, taken off guard and wondering what he was up to—Leslie's warning never far away.

"As opposed to earlier, you mean?" he teased, a gentle smile on his face.

"Sort of."

"My sister warned me to be on my best behavior," Chad said, chuckling as he delivered the soup bowls to the table.

"I'll have to remember to thank her. This is just what I needed after the day I've had. Lucky for me, Leslie's clothes fit. Otherwise, I'd be running around in shorts and t-shirts." For such a horrific day, the evening was shaping up to be a pleasant ending.

Chad shook his head. "Sounds chilly in the middle of a snowstorm."

"Tell me about it." Rachel wanted to set the ground rules since they were stuck here together, ensuring they were on the same page. About everything. "So I thought we should discuss the arrangements since we're both stuck here."

"What's that?" he asked, pausing mid-air with a spoonful of soup.

"Sleeping arrangements." It was easier to tackle the subject head-on and take control, letting him know where she stood.

One eyebrow quirked up, his brow lines deepening. He set his spoon down and sat back in his seat. "What about them?"

"There's only one bedroom, and I'm going to be in it. *Alone*."

"It's my cabin, and you are the guest here, the last time I checked. We have a sofa sleeper that will suit you fine. And absolutely, you will be sleeping alone. There are no worries about that on my account."

With the worst of the arrangements mutually agreed upon, Rachel turned her focus on the bedroom issue. "I want a door that locks—for privacy. I felt sure you would understand. We may be stuck here together, but I've got a reputation to protect."

Chad shook his head. "You've got some nerve relegating me to the sofa, a bed too short for me, I might add, and in my own home. And for the record, my sister's best friend is in a category all by herself that shouts untouchable, and I'm not a peeping Tom."

"I'm sure you'll do fine. You can't possibly have had a queen-size bed everywhere you went when you're deployed. Please?" Rachel asked, tempering her request with kindness, hoping to appeal to his chivalrous side.

"You have a point." Chad nodded, falling silent as they ate their soup.

"This clam chowder is awesome. Did you make it yourself?" she asked, searching for a way to breach the awkward silence.

Chad shook his head. "Hardly. It's from a can. You don't want my cooking, trust me."

"I'm not much better. Cooking was never my thing, but I can get by."

"Good thing we have lots of canned food and frozen food by the sounds of things." Chad shot her a wink.

And just like that, the air was cleared, and some of the day's complex emotions vanished. Leslie was right. Having someone to talk to while she was here wasn't so bad. "Canned food can get old quickly. I said I was not much better, not hopeless," she teased.

"What about bacon and eggs?" Chad asked.

"What about them?"

"For breakfast, your treat."

Rachel thought about it for a few seconds and then relented with a shrug. "Sounds good."

"I look forward to breakfast then," Chad said, standing as he prepared to take his bowl to the kitchen.

"It's a date." She nodded, suddenly looking forward to tomorrow and what it might bring...snowstorm and all. "I'll meet you in the kitchen at seven a.m. sharp."

"Is that when you'll have breakfast on the table like a good wife?" Chad asked, the corners of his eyes crinkling from his broad grin.

His comment stung, but then the big oaf didn't seem overly sensitive to the kind of day she had. Either that, or he had a case of short-term memory. "Hardly. That's when we start cooking breakfast."

Chad shook his head. "Trust me, you want to do this on your own." They moved to rinse the dishes in the sink.

"I do trust you. About as far as I can throw you." Rachel laughed, having fun at his expense. Payback. "I'm sure we can handle it together, and it sounds like it's high time you learned."

Chad seemed like he was about to contradict her, but he suddenly smiled and nodded. "If you say so."

"Why don't you go relax. Maybe tend to the fire or something. You did open a can of soup and heat it, so in all fairness, I reckon I should wash up the dishes."

"Don't forget I heated the bread," he teased.

"That too. Now get out of the kitchen and find something to do." Rachel laughed, tossing the hand towel in Chad's direction.

He caught it as it hit his shoulder and tossed it back, a wide grin on his face. "You don't have to tell me three times. I'm gone." The door swung shut behind him, and Rachel went to work.

The man was incorrigible. And handsome, something she didn't fail to notice. He made her nervous when he turned his smile on her, as smiling wasn't something he did often enough. Chad could be pretty serious at times, as though lost in his own mental world—and not necessarily a place he liked.

Clean-up was simple, and in no time at all, she was finished. Not to mention exhausted from a long and trying day. She found Chad in the living room, staring into the fire, a pensive expression on his face. Lost in his own world again, he hadn't noticed her come into the room.

Rachel turned and headed down the hall, choosing to leave him to a quiet evening.

By the looks of things, it was something they both needed.

Chapter Four

♥

DAYLIGHT PEEKED THROUGH THE cracks in the window curtains, alerting Rachel morning had arrived. A little too early, in her opinion, considering the trouble she had falling asleep. The bed was comfortable, but it was the ominous silence that gave way to more thinking than she wanted in the middle of the night.

Life. Marriage. Alex. Her future. You name it...all the subjects were touched upon as she shifted from side to side, praying to fall into a deep slumber.

Sliding on her slippers, Rachel grabbed the robe off the end of the bed and pulled it on to ward off the early morning chill. Log cabins were beautiful, but the logs absorbed the cool temperatures and dropped the heat inside slightly until the sun warmed them up again.

Rachel moved to the window, yawning along the way. The view that greeted her as she pulled the curtains aside only added to the sensation of cold. The snow was at least four feet deep where the wind whipped into drifts and easily came up to the bottom of her window. And the snowstorm didn't appear to be letting up and was still dumping snow on the mountain.

At this rate, four to five feet seemed like someone erring on the positive side of guessing. All that added up to the realization she wouldn't be leaving the cabin anytime soon. Somehow, she'd make the best of the situation and not worry about it. Besides, worry wouldn't change a thing. Better to bask in the beauty of Mother Nature and use this opportunity to catch up on her Bible studies. To just be. Surely she and Chad could figure out a way to make this snowed-in experience memorable rather than a nightmare.

Rachel brushed her teeth and hair, and then tiptoed down the hallway, being careful so as not to wake Chad. The man was sound asleep on the sofa bed, his feet hanging over the edge. Poor thing didn't look at all comfortable.

A twinge of guilt sliced through her from having ousted him from his own bed in his own home. Perhaps she should offer to switch places. Chad was her best friend's brother, and he seemed harmless enough. Yesterday, her imagination had been a bit overactive. But then, given the day she'd had, it was perfectly normal the way she saw it.

Filling the coffee pot with water, she poured it into the back of the machine. Traditional coffee pots were the norm on the mission trip, not the instant k-cup models that almost every home in America now sported. She added a filter and measured the coffee grounds, counting them spoonful by spoonful and dumping them into the filter. Switching the pot to on, she then sat down at the table and watched the snow coming down, at times, in white-out conditions.

It wasn't long before the aroma of freshly brewed coffee reached her. It kickstarted her body awake even before the first sip, her brain all too aware it meant caffeine was on its way. She waited for the final gurgling sound that signaled it was ready. Then, locating a cup, she poured the coffee, filling it to the top. Raising the cup to her lips tentatively, she took a sip. The last thing she wanted was to burn her mouth with the hot liquid. "*Hmmm*. Just what I needed." She sighed.

"Just what I need, also," Chad said from the doorway.

Startled by his presence, coffee sloshed over the sides of Rachel's cup. She held it out over the sink, trying to catch most of the hot liquid in the basin. "Next time, try not to scare me half to death when you enter a room. That's a cup of precious coffee mostly wasted," she teased. "Not to mention, a mess I need to clean up."

Chad grinned, the lines at the corners of his eyes deepening. "Sorry. I couldn't resist since you were talking to yourself. I figured that instead of an imaginary friend, you could talk to me." The man had an answer for everything.

Rachel reached for a second mug and set it on the counter. She filled the cup and handed it to Chad.

"Thanks. Waking up to the smell of freshly brewed coffee is always an excellent way to start the day. Do you need help—cleaning up, that is?" he asked.

"No, I'm good. It's not much, really, and I was just teasing you because I could."

"I see. I'll have to remember that."

Rachel shot him a grin, topped off her mug and took a sip, and proceeded to search for the paper towels. "I agree about the morning coffee. This is when I like to just sit and relax, gazing out the window and admiring nature's beauty."

Chad turned to glance outside. "Not much to see out there today. And there's no telling when it will move out of here."

"I thought this was supposed to be over and done by now," Rachel said, not entirely saddened by the news now that she had the proper perspective in place.

"It was. But the weather report changed last night right before I went to bed. The storm stalled out because of another high-pressure system. We're now staring at possibly another four feet of snow."

"Another four feet? You've got to be kidding." Rachel knew what the numbers meant, or more importantly, what the total accumulation was adding up to. Eight feet of snow in the space of thirty-six hours. Yikes. Unfortunately, it also meant that at some point, she would have to work on digging her car out before it could even be towed to the garage in town.

"Wish I was kidding, but we're stuck here together for a while," he said, his tone a good indicator he hadn't come to the same conclusion she had last night.

Which reminded her of the resolve to make things right between them. "I'm sure we can come to some arrangement suitable to both of us to make it tolerable. And I'm sorry about taking your room last night. I reckon I should let you have it back, seeing as I *am* the guest," she said, shooting him an apologetic grin.

Chad shook his head. "No. Don't worry about it. I'll make do."

His chivalry and warm generosity were duly noted, and she wasn't about to argue. "Thank you. But if you change your mind, let me know. It's only fair."

"I'm good. Didn't you say something about breakfast this morning?" Chad asked, his stomach rumbling loud enough for Rachel to hear.

She chuckled. "I did. But I also remember telling you it would be a team effort." Rachel wasn't much of a cook, but bacon and eggs...no worries.

He shrugged. "It's an at your own risk thing, but sure." Chad moved to the refrigerator and took out the carton of eggs and the package of bacon. "The bread is in the cupboard," he said, pointing to the door at the far end of the counter.

"Got it." She held up the loaf. "How do you like your eggs?"

"Honestly, anything is fine. Over the years, I've learned to eat what's served or go hungry." Chad grabbed a frying pan and set it on the stove, turning on the burner.

Cutting open the package of bacon, she peeled the strips back, one by one, placing them in the pan. "I'm partial to poached eggs since they are healthier."

"On second thought..." he teased, shooting her a wink. "Poached is fine. On toast, of course."

"Of course." As if there was any other way. Well, there was avocado and poached egg on toast, but that was a treat she left to the fancy breakfast places that now served the popular dish. "Why don't you tend the bacon, and I'll get started on the eggs and toast?" Rachel handed him the spatula.

"Sure thing. Even I can do that." He stood over the frying pan, studying the bacon.

"You might want to turn up the heat. The bacon is not even sizzling yet. It's only going to take me a few minutes to heat up the water and then a few more to cook the eggs and toast. We need to time this right."

"Yes, Chef Rachel." Chad's smile was warm and gentle, as though working in the kitchen with her was a completely natural and normal thing to do. He turned the gas higher on the burner and flipped the bacon.

It was too soon, but she wasn't going to burst his cooking-bubble euphoria. Rachel lit the burner, turning the gas up to high to heat the pot of water. She reached for the plates and set the table, returning to the stove just as the water began to boil.

After pushing down the slot control for the toaster, she started cracking the eggs to drop them in the pot of water. A fancy poached egg maker wouldn't be a staple item in a mountain cabin, and the good old-fashioned way would have to do. One busted, the yolk making the water cloudy. "Well, that one's a lost cause." She frowned.

"Maybe you should go back to Egg 101 class?" Chad teased.

"Maybe so, but you need Bacon 101. The grease is popping everywhere on the stove, and they all need to be flipped before they burn." She gestured toward the bacon, now darkened on one half and close to overdone. *On one side.*

"Bacon sizzles. I'll clean it up after. Maybe that's why you assigned me to this part." Chad flipped a few more pieces. The grease popped and splattered as the strips landed.

"Ouch," Rachel said, jumping back and rubbing the spots where the grease landed on her skin, trying to ease the sting.

"Sorry. Almost finished." He stepped away, retrieving a dish towel, and coming to stand next to her. "Give me your arm."

She did as she was told, knowing it would be useless to argue. "I'm okay. It only stings."

Chad dabbed at the area with a water moistened end of the cloth, the effect cooling. "If you're sure. It doesn't look like it burned the skin."

"I'm sure." Rachel used a ladle to move the poached eggs around. The toast was taking a while but should be close. She peered into the slots just to double-check. "Almost done," she announced.

The grease popped and spattered out of the frying pan again. "*Ummm...*you're getting close to finished. Maybe you should turn down the heat."

Chad frowned. "Maybe? You're the one who said turn it up."

"Well, now I'm telling you to turn it down to finish cooking them. If you don't, we're going to have burnt bacon for breakfast, and I, for one, don't care for it blackened to a crisp."

"Yes, Chef," he teased.

Rachel glanced at the toaster, positive it should have popped by now. The eggs looked ready, but a bit longer would ensure they weren't too runny. She hated the clear whites of a partially cooked egg.

"I'll get us some juice and coffee refills if you can handle finishing up here?" he offered.

"Sure thing. It might be a safer choice if we want to eat this morning," Rachel said, laughing at Chad. Coming to the cabin, she would have never expected to be sharing breakfast with a man. A stranger, no less. Okay, so not a stranger. Her best friend's older brother and a nice guy.

She thought back to high school graduation when he'd shown up for Leslie. Tall and handsome, Rachel couldn't help the sudden crush she felt toward him. His years in the military might have toughened him up, but it had done nothing to extinguish his good looks or charm.

"Earth to Rachel, the bacon's burning!" Chad called out, breaking her out of the past and into the present.

Smoke poured from the pan as it sizzled and popped. Nasty blackened bacon was the result of a trip down memory lane. She shoved the pan off the burner. "I'm sorry. It's not edible at this point." She shook her head.

"Don't worry. The eggs and toast are fine."

Chad was being kind, not rubbing in her failure—or laughing at her for that matter. Rachel grabbed a potholder and took the offending bacon to the garbage can, searching out one of the soup cans to dump the grease into safely.

The smoke alarms sounded, the eerie screech racing down her spine. She spun around just in time to see smoke pouring from the toaster. Rachel yanked the cord out to turn it off, the darn thing never popping. The result—burnt toast. *Just great.*

Chad frantically waved a towel in front of the smoke alarm, trying to silence it.

Rachel pulled the back door open, trying to dissipate some of the smoke. She used a fork and removed the blackened bread, tossing it out the back door with a hard fling. Hopefully, some birds or other critters would enjoy the toast on a cold winter's day.

"Don't worry. The eggs are fine," Chad teased, the alarm still not shutting off.

"It's not funny." Rachel wanted to cry, not laugh.

"Sure it is," Chad said, his face changing to an expression of horror. He raced to the stove, the foamy white suds boiling over the sides.

Which meant the eggs had busted open and were now overcooked. "I'm guessing we don't have eggs either." Talk about humiliation. *Why me, Lord?* Just when she thought she had everything figured out, life threw her another curve. A down cycle she wished would end. First Alex, and now this. "I'm sorry. What a waste of food. I'm not used to cooking on a gas stove. It's way harder to control the temperature, and I made the mistake of thinking it would be easy."

"Nothing ever is. So, we are both bad cooks, that makes us even. You can blame it on the stove, and

I'll blame it on a lack of experience. We're even." Chad winked. He moved to the sink with the pan and poured the water down the drain, dumping the eggs into the trash can.

"What do we do now? Go without breakfast by way of punishment. I'm not sure we need to attempt this again," she said with a shake of her head.

Chad chuckled. "Don't be so melodramatic. There's always cereal. *Cold* cereal with milk. And there's a bag of blueberry muffins." Another example of a man with all the answers.

Rachel nodded. "Sounds good, right about now. You clean, I'll fix breakfast...again."

"Try not to burn our Cheerios," he teased.

"It's not my fault I don't know how to use a gas stove or that your toaster was defective." Defense mode was the best offense when admitting you were a failure—a woman who couldn't cook.

By the time Chad finished cleaning, she had everything ready. She'd set his place setting at the end of the table and hers next to him. The table was made for eight people and sitting at opposite ends seemed too formal. Especially given all they had been through this morning to get to this point. Call it a shared camaraderie, but it was something she enjoyed, even with the catastrophic results.

Rachel took his hand, his silent look of surprise quickly masked as she asked for the food blessing. And, of course, she managed to tack on a little extra request for an end to the snowstorm. Of course, God was in control, but it sure couldn't hurt to put in a good word.

Chad slathered butter on his blueberry muffin and took a bite. "This is good. Thank you."

"Spoken by a hungry man who already acknowledged he'd eat anything." It was her turn to tease him. The truth was the easy banter did make her feel better. So did the food in her belly.

He nodded. "True. You know, we didn't get a chance to talk much last night, but there's something I don't understand. If it's too personal, just tell me to butt out."

"Fire away," she said, unsure of where this would lead.

"Yesterday was supposed to be your wedding day. Instead, you show up here in your dress and said something about being left at the altar. What happened?" Nothing subtle about the question.

Rachel shrugged. "Bottom line…my fiancé didn't bother to show up to our wedding. Nice guy, huh? I guess I should consider myself lucky that Alex didn't wait until we were in front of the pastor and all our guests, and then bolt like a runaway groom down the aisle."

"Do you know why he got cold feet? And why no tears from you? I would have thought to see you with red-rimmed puffy eyes, a gallon of Rocky Road ice cream, and a box of tissues at your side."

"Alex and I weren't suited. The truth is…he preferred the wedding planner. And I, well, I prefer my mission trips and traveling. Yet, even as I rode away from the church, I had an odd sense of relief. It was as though God gave me peace in my heart to know it was for the best."

"Interesting perspective, and not one I necessarily agree with. The same logic could be used in reverse. Why wouldn't God let you know not to say yes in the first place if he never intended for you to marry Alex?" Chad challenged.

It was the same thing Rachel had asked herself at least twenty times since yesterday. "Maybe he did. Sometimes people aren't listening as well as they should. I listened to my parents, his parents, and everyone else who thought our next step was marriage. So we got engaged. I was taken off guard when he asked me in a very public setting. I didn't have time to think it through—and it was just the next logical step, so I said yes."

Rachel couldn't believe she was baring her soul to Chad, but in a way, it was helping her to understand herself. To put into words what happened. She had gotten carried away with the moment, and afterward, had been too afraid to fix it as she didn't want to hurt Alex. The mission trip she'd just accepted at the time had been a Godsend, and from her perspective, exactly what she needed. Time away.

Turned out she was right.

"So how is it that driving away and feeling a sense of peace equates with a message from God that all is well?" Chad asked, pushing his plate back, his gaze intent on her as he tried to understand.

"Peace comes from God, so if I feel peace—it is God's message to me."

Chad shook his head. "But if you're good with the way things turned out and you've found peace with your fiancé's defection, then why did you come here?"

It was a fair question and an easy one to answer. "Your sister thought it best to get away from well-meaning sympathetic people with prying eyes, constantly trying to console me. And my parents, of course. It was meant to give me time to regroup and figure out my next step. Leslie understands my family all too well. I figured while I was here I could apply for more mission trips without my mother's constant interference. It's like a huge weight has been lifted off my shoulders, and I have the freedom to pick where I want to go and what I want to do."

"A change in pace can do that for you. For me, it was coming home. Why mission trips?" Chad asked.

Now, this was a subject Rachel was all too ready to discuss. "I love to help others, bringing cheer to those who need it the most. Ever since I was little, my grandfather used to tell me I was God's little helper. I loved the idea, and it stuck. Fast forward to adulthood, I now understand what he was saying a lot more."

"And what's that?"

"Everyone has gifts from God. It's whether they choose to use them for His glory, or ignore them, that makes the difference. For me, I have the helper gift. It's why helping others brings me so much joy."

"I see, I think, anyway."

Rachel laughed. "Let me put it to you this way. Let's say I tried to be a nurse thinking it was a great career choice and lots of money."

"It would be. Nurses are in high demand," he countered, settling into the back of his chair, his arms across his chest.

"But I don't have a healing gift. Trust me, I've tried. But I've always struggled with the right words to say to someone sick or in the hospital. But tell me they needed their house cleaned or some food shopping done, and I would be happy to jump in and help. Nursing wouldn't fill me with the joy I get from helping others who have a need."

"You didn't get the cooking gift either," he teased, shooting her a wink. Leave it to Chad to bring the conversation full circle.

It was a fair statement, even if it was mocking her. "Ha-ha. But yes, that's sort of my point."

"Seriously, it's great that you know what you want. Any idea where you'd like to go on these mission trips?"

More than he could imagine and more than she'd bore him with. It would take years to see all the places she wanted to visit. But one stood out above all the rest. "Alaska has been my dream, but those spots fill up fast." She'd tried her senior year in high school, and every year after that, but her timing was never good.

"Good place for you to meet one of those hunky men in Alaska, like the ones in the books my sister is always reading." Chad chuckled.

Leslie did love a good romance, but that's where Rachel believed she and her friend were different. Or at least, now she did. "Leslie still has the idea one day she'll meet someone special, and that love might be just around the corner. Your sister is quite a romantic. Me, I think this whole thing with Alex has helped me to understand more about myself. I'm not cut out for a relationship or marriage. My God-given talent is helping others, not wife and mother."

"Good thing, considering you can't cook," he retorted, a huge grin on his face.

"Chad—" It would seem he wasn't about to let this morning's disaster come to a natural death.

"I'm teasing." He covered her hand in his. "And Rachel, I would like to apologize for my marriage comment yesterday. It wasn't nice, especially given the day you had."

"No, it wasn't nice. But thank you." Leslie's brother was A-OK in her books, her crush secretly revived—or at least, the barest smidgeon of it. It was a strange feeling being snowed in with Chad, one that left her wondering more about him and his reasons for showing up unannounced. And if he could ask her questions, there was no reason she couldn't ask him.

Chad made his way to the sink, rinsing the dishes before putting them in the dishwasher.

A man who did dishes was a man after her heart. Not that she wanted a man or anything considering she'd just come out of a relationship. Traveling around the world was her next exciting adventure. Still, if she was looking for romance—Chad McCarthy would undoubtedly have interested her.

Chapter Five

♥

T HE SNOW STILL HADN'T stopped falling, and the wind was kicking up. Which was a good thing if it jumpstarted the storm front to move north. Rachel didn't relish digging her car out. But when the time came, she hoped Chad might lend a hand.

The days leading up to the wedding had been fraught with completing last-minute details, and Rachel had missed out on some of the more in-depth Bible study time she enjoyed. With plenty of hours at her disposal and nothing to do, it was the perfect opportunity to dive in. Not to mention, reading God's word always left her with a sense of joy and contentment. She chose to stay in her bedroom, giving Chad plenty of space. It's not like he planned on company when he first arrived, and she knew he had work to do.

Thinking about her conversation with Chad, she chose peace as the topic of today's readings. His comments had left her wondering about his relationship with God, but she wouldn't pry. Long ago, she'd learned being a light to others meant being true to herself, letting her faith reflect the joy in her life.

The morning passed much faster than she expected. The Bible had 329 verses where the word peace appeared, and Rachel found every one of them, reading the words out loud and soaking in their meaning. She stood and stretched, a big yawn escaping as she pushed back the lazy sleepiness clouding her brain.

Rachel went in search of Chad but didn't find him anywhere in the cabin. Glancing out the kitchen window, a movement in the backyard caught her attention. It would seem Chad had dug out the snow around the woodpile and was loading logs in a carry-bag. He picked it up, effortlessly hoisting the straps over his shoulder and headed for the cabin.

She moved away from the window, not wanting to be caught watching.

Chad looked up as he entered through the back door, stomping his feet on the mat to get rid of the snow. "It's cold out there," he said, setting the bag down and brushing the snow off his jacket.

"I can tell. Your cheeks are bright red." She smiled, reaching for the wood, intent on taking it to the fireplace. "I'll take this in."

"It's heavy. I'll get it in a second," Chad said, sitting down on the chair to untie his boots.

Rachel lifted the bag and promptly set it down. It was heavier than she expected, not that she'd admit it to Chad. "Okay, Mr. Macho Man, have it your way. Do you want some hot cocoa?" she asked. "I'm sure you don't mind me doing the little-lady activities." Rachel grinned, unable to fight back the natural urge to taunt the guy. She could give as good as he did if she found her tongue in time, that is. Usually, the conversation had ended long before the perfect retort came to mind.

"I'm not sure. I like my cocoa brown, not black. Think you can manage not to burn it?"

The teasing light in his eyes was endearing and made it entirely impossible to take offense. "The man makes a good point, but I think I can handle fixing you cocoa. Unless you're offering to do it?"

Chad picked up the firewood. "Have at it. Call it a chance at redemption. But for lunch, let's stick to sandwiches and canned goods. I'm hungry and don't have time for do-overs." He chuckled as he headed toward the living room.

"Don't push your luck, mister. Cocoa coming right up. And I'll see what Chef Campbell is cooking up today," she joked, having fun even though the joke was on her.

"Now you're talking. Tomato is one of my favorites."

Rachel nodded. "Lucky for you, it's mine also. That and buttered bread. Yum." Of course, her mother thought the canned soup wasn't fit for the table, but luckily, Rachel's grandfather hadn't felt the same, and the two shared many cans of soup over the years. Fond memories, like tomato soup and grilled cheese sandwiches in an igloo they built together.

Chad paused and frowned. "That's extra unnecessary carbs."

"Mine to count," she retorted.

"That's true. Buttered bread it is since I just hauled in wood. I think I can afford a few extra carbs myself. Oh, and on second thought, skip the cocoa. Chocolate and tomatoes are not a combination that sounds like they would sit well in my stomach. Then I'd have to blame your cooking if I got sick," he said, his eyes crinkling as he grinned.

Rachel shook her head. "Are you ever going to let me live down our burnt breakfast?"

"Probably not. It's a fun memory, something I've had precious little of lately." Chad walked out of the room.

It was just as Rachel expected. Chad had some deep-seated issues that were troubling him. His cryptic comment was concerning, and over lunch, she intended to find out more. She'd already told Chad her gift was that of a helper, and instinctively she knew he needed help. But how far did one press for information before it was considered crossing the line into an invasion of someone's privacy? It was a delicate balance, but one she had to aim for.

Rachel fixed lunch, stirring the soup constantly, unwilling to let anything go wrong. She wasn't help-less in the kitchen, not by a long shot. This morning was simply a case of what could go wrong—did.

After pouring the soup into the bowls, she buttered and cut two slices of bread, arranging them around the sides of the plate. Then, she carried them to the living room, careful to not let the bowls slide off. That was a disaster she absolutely couldn't bear to happen.

She found Chad sitting by the fire and reading a book.

He looked up as she approached, coming to his feet. "Let me help," he said, reaching for the tray and setting it down on the coffee table.

"Thanks. I splurged and did two slices for each of us. Watch out for calories. Now, if we have turkey soup, it's another matter entirely. Then we must have buttered crackers." She laughed.

Chad had pulled out two TV trays, which made it easier to eat. Sitting across from each other made the setting cozier, the firelight dancing in the room. Rachel was surprised when he looked up at her. "I'll let you ask the blessing."

Pleased he remembered, Rachel couldn't help but wonder if he would even volunteer to be the one to pray one of these times. She bowed her head and asked a short blessing, not one to keep a man and his meal apart. Especially not a hungry man. Too many times, people prayed, and by the time they finished, the food was cold. Their hearts were in the right place, but they used the opportunity to deliver a message instead of a blessing since they had a captive audience.

When she finished, Chad picked up his spoon and started to eat.

"*Hmmm*. Now this hits the spot. *You can cook.*" He grinned.

"I can. Soup is always easy, so you're safe."

They fell silent, each more than a little hungry. Rachel tried to get up the nerve to ask him questions about his life in order to find out more about what was troubling him. *A burden shared was half the load.*

She took a deep breath. "You asked about why I was here and I answered. I think it's only fair that you share your story, given that Leslie thought you were still in Afghanistan. This return home must have been a recent development."

Chad frowned, but then visibly relaxed. "I've only been back a few days. Leslie didn't know because I wanted to be alone and enjoy the quiet. No offense."

"None taken." It was true. Rachel had suddenly landed on his doorstep and she'd been forced to stay at the cabin. So far, he'd been fairly gracious about the whole thing.

He nodded. "If Leslie knew I was here, she would have barged in and started lining me up with activities. I'm just not ready for that. It's a big adjustment getting out of the military."

"Oh, I didn't realize this was an out, like a permanent out. I thought you were on leave. And I'm sure you're right about Leslie. She is always on the go. But I also know how much she's missed you." Rachel smiled. "So why did you get out?" She knew she was pressing her luck asking for more information, but she had to try.

Chad leaned back in his seat, gazing into the fire. "My contract was up, and I wanted something different."

"I thought people in for as long as you were, become lifers. You know, like retire from the military."

"They do. But sometimes things happen that change your mind." His tone had grown distant.

Now they were getting somewhere. "Like what?"

"War isn't pretty on any level. And you can't unsee what you've seen." Chad rose and moved to stand in front of the fire, his gaze trained on the flames as they licked higher when he added a log.

"I'm sorry." It sounded lame and didn't begin to cover the multitude of things she should say. She was usually good at this, but with Chad, his wounds appeared deep. This might be something way over her pay grade, more like something a professional counselor needed to handle.

"It's all good," he said, turning to face her. He was clearly trying to sound more upbeat. It was as though he'd retreated to some dark world and suddenly resurfaced. "I started working over at the community center building, trying to get it fixed up and reopened. I'm renovating the space to implement a kid's program I intend to make a reality."

"That sounds wonderful. What type of program?" Rachel asked, totally interested and not just because of the change it brought about in Chad.

"It's for the children of missing or deceased soldiers. It'll be a sport and crafting camp, with the bonus of tutors being available to help with school deficiencies. Anything that adds joy to a kid's life who feels the light is missing after losing a parent. These kids are at risk and need someone to make sure they stay on track. It's an idea I've been thinking about and planning for over a year. When my contract came up for renewal, I decided the time to put it into action was now, so I didn't re-up." Chad's voice had become animated, his passion for the project undeniable.

"What a great idea. Does that mean you're planning on staying here permanently now?"

"I am. I've had my fill of traveling around the world."

The finality of his comment seemed to pull him back into the dark place he went at times. A place she didn't want to leave him. "But there is so much beauty in the world…the other side of what you saw."

Chad shook his head. "For me, there is no other side."

"That's a sad way to feel about life. There is so much kindness if one is paying attention. It's what I see on the mission trips—people helping people. No matter their differences, or language barriers, or culture, people work together for the greater good."

He returned to his seat. "Your world, not mine. Eat up, your soups getting cold."

In other words, end of discussion.

Rachel's heart went out to him, but she was positive he wouldn't appreciate her saying so. Chad had been a tough military soldier, and now he was a tough civilian. She sensed there was way more to his story, information he clearly had no intention of revealing.

They ate the rest of the meal in awkward silence. Rachel stood at the same time as Chad, picking up her plate. "I'll take these to the kitchen and rinse them off. Then, if you're interested, you could set up the game of Life, and we could play, if you're not afraid of losing, that is." Rachel wanted to tease him back to a happy place.

"What about Stratego? Life is a little too girlie-girl for me, with all the marriage, kids, insurance, college, and financial elements added in." Chad grinned, joining in the fun.

She was impressed. Life wasn't a game she would have expected him to know anything about. "Fine. Just because you are a military guy, doesn't mean you'll beat me. I'm quite good at the game, and last I heard, you are ex-military," Rachel teased as she headed for the kitchen, her eyes twinkling in merriment.

"Former military," he corrected. "And I've still got moves."

"We'll see about that," she shot back the parting remark before disappearing into the kitchen to finish rinsing the dishes.

It didn't take long and she rejoined Chad, where he'd set up the game on the coffee table, placing cushions on the floor as seats. It was all very cozy by the roaring fire. She sat down, turning the board around and picking up the box of pieces on his side of the table.

"Why do you get red?" he asked.

"Because you said you've got moves, and therefore, I should get the benefit of going first." Rachel chuckled as she began setting up the pieces.

"Fair enough." Chad didn't take nearly as long as she did, the man knowing which piece he wanted and where to put it.

Rachel pondered over the placement, trying to put her bombs in strategic places, all while protecting her high-ranking officers. Finally, after moving them around several times, she was ready. "All set?" Rachel asked, knowing he was, but making sure. She wouldn't want to make a move and have him start adjusting his pieces again.

"Ready. May the best strategizer win." Chad laughed, his smile crinkling the corners of his eyes.

Years in the sun had added lines to his face, but they didn't detract from his good looks. If anything, they were more like lines of maturity, something she appreciated.

Move after move, they advanced and retreated on the board, calling out the rank of the pieces when they clashed. The lowest valued player won the battle, but it also alerted the other team to what you had on the spot, allowing them to figure out how to go after and eliminate the piece on the board.

Chad landed on one of her squares. "Four," he called out.

"Seven."

He plucked her piece off the board, grinning.

Rachel took her turn, choosing not to clash this time but instead to move a piece away from the center of the board, where Chad was determined to advance. She held her breath, waiting to see his next move.

He picked up his four, but then set it back down again.

Drat. Rachel wanted him to move it forward, knowing she had a surprise waiting for him if he did.

Chad looked up at her, a gleam in his eye. "I wonder if this is a safe piece. You haven't moved him yet, but I don't think you would put a bomb up in the front away from your flag." He watched her closely.

Rachel forced herself to remain expressionless, not wanting to give anything away.

He picked up the four again and moved it forward. "Four."

"Bomb!" She shouted, jumping to her feet, and twirling around in a happy dance.

A deafening explosion sounded as glass shattered.

Rachel screamed and turned, watching as a large tree branch came to rest in the front room, not more than fifteen feet from them.

"You didn't have to bomb my house," Chad said, trying to lighten the moment as he drew her near and held her tight.

Rachel couldn't stop shaking, the realization of how close they'd come to being crushed sinking in.

"It'll be okay, Rachel. We're fine and that's all that matters. I noticed the tree when I arrived and that it was leaning, but I didn't have time to take care of it yet."

"It's a mess. And it's letting all the cold air and snow in the cabin. We've got to do something," Rachel said, pulling herself together.

"Are you okay to help me?"

"Of course, just tell me what to do, Mr. Military man with the moves." Rachel's sense of humor had returned, even if her heart was still racing.

"If you can sweep up the glass, I'll get a chainsaw. We've got to cut this part out of here and then seal the gap with plastic. With any luck, there will be some boards in the shed I can tack up. Otherwise, it's going to get mighty cold in here tonight."

Chad was taking charge of the situation, and Rachel was totally onboard with letting him. "I'll get right on it. Fingers crossed on the boards, as cold doesn't sound like much fun."

"Luckily, we have the fire and plenty of wood. I can keep it burning all night if needed for extra heat."

"Sounds good, although maybe we can take turns on fire vigil," she offered, more than willing to do her part. Teamwork was always a good thing in her book.

Chad paused at the door. "I wouldn't say no. Working together will help make all of this less of a problem."

Rachel headed for the kitchen pantry to get the broom and dustpan, grabbing her jacket to put on as she passed the closet. The temperatures inside were dropping fast with the giant gaping hole where the window used to be, and the blowing snow had started to lay a white film on the floor.

Side by side, the two of them worked at it for over an hour. Chad had the worst end of it, having to work outside as he cut away the branch. She at least had the warmth of the fire behind her. Rachel emptied the last glass shards and sticks into the wastebasket, glancing around to ensure no slivers were missed. Then, just to be safe, she decided to make a full sweep of the area one last time.

"Rachel, can you come and grab the other end of this plastic sheet and pull tight. I'm going to use the staple gun to tack it into place," Chad called out.

She pulled off her gloves, more than ready to help. "Sure thing." This wasn't the time to dwell on the cold. Soon enough, the inside of the cabin would warm up again, and that's what she needed to focus on. They were blessed to have all they needed on hand and that the electricity hadn't gone out. The Lord hadn't given them more than they could handle, and she sent up a silent prayer of thanks.

Rachel shivered as she held onto the plastic. Bit by bit, Chad closed the gap, the snow and the cold winds no longer blowing into the house.

He moved to stand next to her. "You're freezing. Why don't you go warm up by the fire and let me finish up by hanging the boards outside? It won't take me long."

"I won't say no," she said, repeating Chad's earlier comment. Her fingers were frozen, and the heat would be a welcome relief.

Chad headed outside, drill and a box of screws in hand. It wasn't long before he was back inside and joined her by the fire. "All done," he said, shrugging out of his coat. "Until the storm passes and I can get into town, that is."

"Thank goodness." She breathed a sigh of relief and tried to relax.

"Let me see your fingers," he said, reaching for her hands. "They were turning white earlier, and I was worried about frostbite."

"They're almost back to normal. I've got Raynaud's disease, and it doesn't take much for them to turn white. It's when they turn blue I start to worry." She was trying to alleviate his concern, but Rachel rather liked that not only had he noticed, but that he cared.

Chad brought her hands to his face, cupping them in his as he blew gently and rubbed, the combination restoring her circulation almost instantly.

Suddenly a little nervous and a lot of shy, Rachel tried to pull her hands away. "Thank you."

Chad hadn't let go of her hands as he stood there, his gaze watching her intently. The moment stretched out, neither one moving. Was there something on her face? Something he wanted to say, but hesitated? Or did he want to kiss her?

She moved away, suddenly uncomfortable. They'd just worked together as a team, laughing and shivering, but getting the job done. It was a shared memory she wouldn't soon forget. A moment when the military man let down his guard and showed genuine friendship laced with care and concern. The same care and concern he wanted to show the children who had lost a parent in the military.

But none of that changed the facts. Rachel was ready to travel the world, and Chad was prepared to settle down. She would be ten times the fool if she let herself care for him. They both had the same end goal—helping people, but their paths differed in how to carry out those goals.

"I'll go fix you some coffee; you deserve it," she said, using it as the first excuse that came to mind in order to leave the room, needing a quiet place to reflect on her feelings.

She had just gained newfound freedom, something she wouldn't give up easily. Not even for Leslie's handsome brother.

Chapter Six

♥

Pouring herself a cup of coffee, Rachel gazed out the kitchen window. Chad was out by the shed, digging out the entryway. He must have been up for a while if he was already outside working. It suddenly dawned on her the snow had finally stopped coming down.

White snow glistened, fresh and untrodden, the shiny, smooth surface pristine. Rachel couldn't wait to get outside, anxious to capture Mother Nature as it reawakened to the rays of sunshine warming the area. Wildlife would creep out of hiding to explore and find food. The birds would flutter about, calling out to each other in the joy of the new day.

Rachel sipped the hot brew, readjusting to the bolder flavor Chad tended to make when he got up first.

It wasn't long before Chad had the double doors of the shed opened, and he disappeared inside. When he reappeared, she was more than a little surprised to see him tugging a sled.

Picturing him gliding down a mountainside and laughing all the way made Rachel grin. This was a boyish side she hadn't known existed. He headed toward the cabin, and Rachel moved away from the window. She hadn't gone sledding in forever, and her own inner excitement started to build, hoping he would ask her to join him.

Chad stomped his boots on the back porch and came inside, the brisk cold air with him.

Rachel pulled her sweater tighter to ward off the chill. "You're up early," she said as he removed his coat and hat.

"I was. Shortly after five, which wasn't exactly on my agenda. Thought I'd take advantage of the time to start digging us out."

"Sounds like a good idea. I haven't even finished my first cup of coffee."

"Get a move on, woman. I found my old toboggan, and we should hit the hills. There are some great ones around here. If you dare, that is," he taunted.

It didn't matter if he hadn't issued the challenge; she wouldn't have missed a chance to sled for anything. "Oh, I dare, don't you worry. Just let me eat something and suit up, and then let's have at it."

"A woman who faces a challenge head-on. Nice. I'll pack us lunch while you get ready."

Rachel frowned. "Lunch? I'm just having breakfast."

"I know. But by the time we walk to the best hill around, go sledding, and get back, it will be lunchtime. I figure if we work up a hunger, we could eat and then walk back." He tossed his jacket on the chair nearby.

"That sounds reasonable. I'll grab a protein bar and get changed. Hopefully, Leslie has a snowsuit here."

"Be sure to check the hall closet." He pointed to the door that opened off the front entry. "But if not, I've got an extra pair of snow pants and a coat you can wear."

Picturing herself in Chad's outdoor wear wasn't flattering. "I would more than likely look like the abominable snowman in anything that fits you," she said with a shake of her head.

"Nah, more like a grizzly bear. It's black," Chad teased.

Rachel frowned. "Let's just hope Leslie has something. I think she'd kill me if I ruined her lavender pea coat." She headed into the kitchen, grabbed a breakfast bar, and headed down the hall, excited to be able to get out and have some fun. And sledding ranked high on her list. Of course, sledding with Chad moved it to the top of the list, but it wasn't anything she would bother to mention to her best friend. Some things were best kept under wraps if Rachel didn't want to play twenty questions with Leslie. And if her friend started down the matchmaking road, it would only make everything more complicated. Not to mention, Rachel was already having trouble with her own view of Chad. She found herself liking him, despite his prickly outer shell that popped up occasionally.

Fifteen minutes later, she was ready to go and went in search of Chad.

He grinned when he spotted her, the deep grooves in his cheeks proof he was trying to hold back his laughter. "You said something about the abominable snowman, and it looks like you guessed right. Although the pink scarf does downplay the image."

"It's all she had here. Miss Fashion must have all her good clothes in town."

"You can say that again," he teased.

Chad was right, but she wouldn't give him the satisfaction of knowing she agreed. "Enough. It's getting hot in this snowsuit. Let's go."

"I just need to throw on my coat and boots. Meet you out back." Chad picked up his coat as Rachel headed out the door.

She sucked in the cold air, welcoming the relief from the heated temperatures trapped in the suit. Picking up a ball of snow, she took a bite. Clean and refreshing. When they got back to the cabin, Rachel wanted to check the cupboards for vanilla and evaporated milk. Snow cream would be a delicious treat. It was always something she looked forward to each year, and the first snow was always special.

Of course, the old wives' tale was to not use the first snow of the season as it was thought to clean the air. But with eight feet of snow that dumped, surely the snow would be clean at the top, and she didn't intend to dig to the bottom. Rachel grinned when she spotted a bunny running from tree to tree. She pulled off one of her gloves and retrieved her phone from the front pocket of the snowsuit, intent on trying to capture the moment.

Chad came outside, managing to scare the rabbit away just as she got the camera focused, leaving her no time to get the shot off.

"Good timing, mister," she teased as he drew near.

"What was it?"

Rachel pouted. "A bunny. I love pictures of wildlife, and he was so cute."

"How do you know the bunny wasn't a she?"

"I don't. But the English language allows the term *he* to be used when one is unsure. It's a generically accepted word."

"Okay, Miss Grammarly. I promise there will be more bunnies. We've always been overrun by the furry critters. I reckon more so now, what with the cabin vacant lately."

"Yay. Everywhere I go, I take pictures of birds and wildlife. There's just something so peaceful watching them flitter about in their natural environment." She glanced around, hoping Chad was right.

"I agree with you. I'm more about the animals than the birds, but for the same reason. So see, we do have something in common." He shot her a dazzling smile that filled her with a special warmth.

"You mean besides the fact we both can't cook," she teased, enjoying their camaraderie, even if it wouldn't last much longer. They both had agendas, and life would go on after the effects of the snowstorm were cleaned up.

"There is that, but I was referring to a positive characteristic. The inability to cook is not something we should let get out willy-nilly," Chad said, his grin ear to ear.

Her eyebrows shot up. "Wow. Willy-nilly? Did you really just say that?"

Chad nodded. "I did. Why?"

"It's something my grandmother used to say." Rachel chuckled, the memory a sweet one.

"Sounds like a smart woman."

"She was at that, and she loved her old colloquialisms. It was a way to keep the past in the present, is what she always told me."

"Nice. Shall we go?" Chad pointed to a place where the trees parted like welcoming gates into the forest.

Rachel frowned. "I'm not sure I'll get very far. Do you see how deep this is? I mean, you shoveled it. We will sink right in." She'd gotten excited about nothing, or so it would seem.

Chad laughed. "Which is exactly why I laid out those," he said, pointing at the shed and two pairs of snowshoes she hadn't noticed before.

"Except I don't have a clue how to use them."

"Think of them as oversized web feet. Leslie's snowshoes will fit you nicely, and you shouldn't have any trouble. Just go slow at first until you get the hang of it. I wouldn't want you to land a face plant," he explained.

"It's not high on my priority list either. Fine. Hand them to me and I can try." Rachel took the snowshoes from Chad and then watched as he laced them on. She mimicked his actions and, in no time, was ready to try walking. She took a step and wobbled, unsure of herself.

"It's better in the deep snow. Here take my hand, and I'll help you get over the bank," Chad offered.

She took his hand, grateful for the support. The wall was high where he'd cleared out the snow, but in one section, he'd tapered it as if he planned this outing. Which, by all intents and purposes, it looked like he had, judging by the food pack he carried. "Thank you."

"My pleasure."

Rachel took a few steps, and with Chad's support, managed quite well.

"Good job. I'm going to grab the sled. Why don't you practice walking around now that we are on level ground?" he suggested.

"Okay." Mustering her courage, she boldly took a step. And then another. And another. It wasn't as hard as she thought it would be. In fact, it was like walking in swim fins, something she was far more familiar with. Except in swim fins, one was supposed to walk backward, so from that perspective, this was easier.

"You're doing great," Chad called out from behind her.

Rachel turned and smiled. "Than—*ohhh*," she squealed as one snowshoe trapped the other and sent her flying forward, her arms shooting forward to brace against the fall.

"Well, almost," he teased as she sat up, sputtering, and wiping the snow from her face.

"That was your fault. You distracted me." Rachel gathered up a snowball and tossed it at Chad.

He ducked, and the snowball missed. "Whatever you say. I'll take the blame, seeing as one of us has to since we're a team."

"Since when are we a team?" she asked, holding up her hand for Chad to help pull her back to her feet.

"Since today," he said, successfully getting her upright. "This is a toboggan," he pointed at the sled, "and there are two of us."

"Oh, I see. I thought it was a solo thing." She hadn't ridden a toboggan, and the idea of speeding down the hill by herself was intriguing but not particularly her first choice. His idea sounded far better.

"Nope, we need to work together if we don't intend to crash. You do know how to sled, right?"

"Of course. But I want to be in the front."

"Why is that?" Chad asked, his face scrunched as he questioned her motive.

"So I can see where we're headed. If we're going to crash into a tree, I want to be able to eject myself from the sled." Rachel grinned.

Chad shook his head. "Better still, you help me steer away from the tree, so we both avoid crashing into said tree and not suffer an injury."

"I suppose," she teased.

It wasn't long before Rachel got her snowshoe feet in sync, and she was soon comfortable enough to glance around. The natural beauty of a mountain freshly covered in snow was awe-inspiring.

They hadn't gone far when Rachel spotted another bunny. She stopped, holding up her hand to signal Chad to do the same. She pointed in the animal's direction. "Look, there are two of them." Rachel pulled off her gloves, pressing them between her knees. She pulled out her camera and snapped off a few quick shots, hoping to get a couple of pictures before she played with the settings. Adjusting the zoom and lighting to capture the playful critters in a more enhanced manner took more time than one could predict you had with wildlife.

Rachel laughed when one toppled over the other. "Aren't they cute?" she asked, turning to Chad.

"You are." He chuckled. "I've never seen anyone quite so into getting the perfect bunny shot. Next thing you know, you'll be asking them to pose."

"Laugh now, mister. But wait until you see the photos." The perfect shot, perfect lighting, perfect everything, took time. Time Rachel was willing to commit for the right photo.

"I'll do that. I'm having more fun watching you."

His comment gave Rachel an unexpected rush of delight. She preferred not to dwell on the reasoning behind the emotion. "How much further?" she asked, trying to deflect the moment.

"Not far now."

"Good. This walking on snow is way more tiring than I expected. A sled ride downhill will be a welcome relief."

"Yes, but then we have to walk back up the hill."

"*Ugh*, don't remind me," she said, the idea daunting.

"If it's too much, we could always circle back to the cabin from the bottom of the hill. One direction is always way more fun."

Chad was her guide for the morning, and whatever he suggested, she was more than willing to go along with. "I already like the sound of that. As long as this isn't some bunny hill you've dragged me out to see."

"Hardly a bunny trail. Trust me. Although bunnies seem to be your specialty," Chad teased. "Consider this more of a Black Diamond trail."

Rachel stopped in her tracks. "*Ummm*, should I be worried?" A bunny trail might not be so bad after all.

"Nope. I've done it plenty of times. Leslie wasn't big into sledding, but I was. I always made it back to my uncle's cabin." A distant gaze fell over his expression. One second he was laughing and having fun, and the next, his mood turned a one-eighty.

Rachel felt sure it had to do with the make-it-home comment, but it was better not to draw attention to the remark. This was a fun outing, and she didn't want anything to intrude upon the day negatively. Especially not before they careened down the mountain. "So I see," she said, aiming for a light-hearted teasing note. "I can't wait to see your idea of a challenging hill."

"Take a look," he said. "We're here."

Rachel huffed several large vapor clouds as she tried to catch her breath from the exertion of the hill. "This is incredible, and *ummm*, very steep. Maybe I should watch." It wasn't anything like what she expected. At the ski resorts, tube trails were wide open and well-groomed. Unfortunately, neither term applied to the path they would need to take down the side of the mountain.

"Chicken?" he teased, putting the toboggan down at the precipice of the hill and holding it in place with his foot.

This was way more than anything she'd ever done. "No, a bunny." It was a feeble attempt to diffuse her nerves.

"And here I thought you were going for an abominable snowman."

The guy never let up with the jokes, something Leslie had warned her about. Rachel picked up a handful of snow, sculpted it into a snowball, and tossed it at Chad, catching him by surprise.

"Hey, no fair." He reciprocated and fired one off toward her, the snowball landing against her chest.

The time for rest was over. Rachel moved further away and tossed a few more snowballs in his direction. One of them landing squarely against his chest. Chad dropped the toboggan rope and chased after her. And by chase, she meant an awkward gorilla run. One that was over before she knew it as he tackled her to the ground.

Picking up a handful of snow, he held it above her face. "Truce," he asked.

Rachel was caught up in the moment, breathless from the exertion, and Chad's gorgeous face and chocolatey eyes so close to hers. A brief flash of time in which neither moved, assessing, and reassessing the situation.

A hawk screeched in the distance, breaking the silence and the moment.

"Truce," she said, exhaling. There was plenty more she might have said, except the words wouldn't come.

Chad stood, lending her a hand up. "You ready to do this?"

"As long as you know how to steer this thing, I am. I'm trusting you with my life."

"I'll take good care of you, I promise." Chad reset the toboggan in place and held out his hand.

Rachel allowed him to help her sit on the sled while she removed her snowshoes and handed them to him to put in the backpack. He'd already ditched his and was ready to go. She faced the front and waited while he got into position behind her. From this viewpoint, the hill looked even steeper, and her fear ramped up another notch. Or two.

She'd meant it when she said she trusted Chad. But right now, that trust wasn't giving her the confidence she needed to pick up her feet and put them on the sled. Rachel looked to the heavens above. *Please, God, keep us safe and give me the courage to face this challenge with bravery and trust, both in You and Chad.*

A cardinal landed on a tree nearby, his beautiful red coloring a stark contrast to the green and white all around. Joy and peace filled Rachel, and she understood the message. Everything would be okay.

"Let's do this," she said, pulling her legs in to cross them in front. She clung to the ropes on the side of the toboggan.

"Here we go. It'll be fun, so remember to open your eyes." Chad chuckled.

Seconds later, they were careening down the mountainside. The cold air made Rachel's eyes water, and she squeezed them tight, hoping to clear her vision. There was no way she was letting go of the side ropes. To the right. A quick left. Another left. Dodging the trees, Chad was as experienced as he claimed, the man quite able to steer the sled easily.

Soon, she was enjoying the ride, even relaxing just enough to use the back of her glove to brush the tears off her cheeks.

"This is great," she hollered.

"Told you."

They reached the bottom, and Chad dug in his heels, and they came to a stop.

"Can we do it again?" she asked, the thrill of the ride keeping her on an emotional high.

Chad nodded. "Sure thing, but only if you can walk back up." He pointed toward the top where they'd started from.

Rachel zeroed in on the trail they'd cut coming down and on how steep the hill appeared when looking at it from the bottom. "*Ummm*, maybe not. I like the idea of another run, but I'm not sure I can get up the hill on snowshoes or in boots."

"Good call. I wasn't planning on it anyway." He winked.

"Thanks a lot. Making me feel like a weakling."

"Just testing your determination. Shall we?" Chad asked, holding out his hand to help her up.

"Absolutely," she agreed, taking his hand.

Chad positioned the sled, opened his pack, and showed her how to sit, making a table between them. It was like an intimate dinner for two, with only the snow and the birds and Mother Nature to see the moment. And God.

The thought was confusing. Rachel thought God's clear plan for her life was the mission field as a helper. So why was he testing her with the likes of Chad McCarthy? Someone who also had the helper gift, but someone who had completely different ideas on using those God-given gifts to their best use.

Lunch turned out to be a ham and cheese sandwich and warm tomato soup in a thermos, and incredibly delicious, hitting her hunger spot precisely right.

"So tell me about your last mission trip? I mean, what does that look like for you?" Chad asked, handing her a cup of warm cocoa.

"I was in South America for a year. I loved working with kids who were looking to learn about God while at the same time teaching them in school. There are a lot of remote villages that don't have access to any formal education. So the children are eager to learn and soak up the love of God." She took a sip of the creamy hot chocolate. The meal couldn't have been more perfect, but then perhaps it was the company she kept that made it seem that way. It also hadn't escaped her notice that Chad had fixed her the same meal he once protested against. It was proof he'd enjoyed it, contrary to what he'd claimed.

"Sounds awesome. It takes someone with a big heart to give up their life and to travel for such a long period, giving of themselves to others."

Rachel shrugged. "For me, it's more about a love for God. And in that, the love trickles down to the children and those eager to learn. I meet some incredible kids. That's why I'm so excited, knowing that I'll be back out in the field soon." The joy on the child's face was priceless, and it was that emotion Rachel tapped into.

"I see. Have you heard anything yet?" Chad asked, pouring himself another cup of cocoa.

"No, but I will. I'm not sure where my journey will take me, but I know patience is a virtue. How's the community center coming along?"

"Slow. Two steps forward, one step backward. I'll get there but cutting through the red tape has its headaches." Chad polished off his sandwich with one big bite.

"I'm sorry. Just stick with it, and then one day, you'll look back and be able to remember the planning stages fondly."

"I hope you're right." Chad repacked the trash as she finished the last of her lunch. He slid on the backpack, clearly ready to leave.

Rachel stood. "It's a good thing you know your way around. I'd be lost out here."

"I spent too many summers out here not to know my way around." They strapped on their snowshoes.

"Lead the way," she said, ready to leave.

"Okay, then." He picked up the rope, pulling the toboggan behind him as they headed through the trees.

Rachel followed, staying back far enough not to trip over the sled.

They hadn't gone far when he came to a bend, the trees narrowing. He reached up to grab a branch, sending a load of snow cascading down on his head.

"Of course," he said, brushing the snow out of his face.

Rachel lost no time pulling out her phone and snapping a picture, his expression priceless. "Fate," she teased.

"Fate? I don't think so. If you had walked ahead of me, it would have been you."

Rachel laughed as he dusted off the top of his head. "But I didn't. I think it's payback because you laughed at me when I fell. So now it's my turn for a good chuckle."

"Gee, thanks." He shook his head, not finding the humor she did. Or at least none he was willing to let her know.

"No problem. Smile for the camera." Rachel snapped off several more photos instantly with a burst shot.

"No pictures," he said, holding up his hand to block his face.

"Too late." She chuckled, tucking her phone safely out of his reach as he tried to grab it with his other hand. "Let's go, mister. I'm hoping there's snow cream and more cocoa back at the cabin. I'm getting cold now that we haven't been moving much."

"Lucky for you," he quipped.

"Why's that?"

Chad's grin revealed crow's feet at the corners of his eyes. "Otherwise, I might have had to reciprocate the snow dousing." He reached his hand up as if to grab one of the branches.

"You wouldn't dare." She took a step back, unsure if she was right.

"I would dare, but I won't do it. Not this time, any-way." He shot her a wink.

"Not any time, I hope."

"We shall see. By the looks of things, you won't be out of here for at least a few days. Plenty of time for something to happen."

Always the prankster, apparently. Hopefully she'd be gone sooner than later, and Chad wouldn't get a chance.

Chapter Seven

♥

THE MOON SHONE THROUGH the window, casting shadows on the wall. Rachel glanced at the digital clock, its glowing red numbers announcing it was only 2:30. "Ugh," she ground out, rolling to the other side, hoping to find a new comfortable position. Unfortunately, it wasn't even close to time to get out of bed.

Yesterday's sledding expedition left her muscles sore, and she desperately wished she would have done a soaking hot bath after dinner. But between snow cream, hot cocoa, dinner, and a warm fire, all shared with Chad, she'd been loath to give up the relaxing evening.

Her throat was dry. Having forgotten to put a glass of water on the nightstand as was her norm, she flopped the blankets back. The room was cold as she slid on her slippers and robe. Using the moonlight to make her way to the door, she pulled it open and moved down the hallway slowly, trying not to wake Chad as she headed for the kitchen.

Using the flashlight from her cell phone, she took a glass out of the cabinet and filled it with water. A noise caught her attention, and Rachel froze. It sounded like a wounded animal. She glanced out the window but saw nothing, clouds blocking the moonlight. The eerie sound repeated, except this time she recognized that it came from within the cabin.

Rachel moved out of the kitchen, nervously glancing around. She started down the hall, the sound coming from behind her this time.

Chad? She moved back toward the living room and discovered him thrashing about on the sofa bed, his blankets flung off.

"*No. No. There's a bomb,*" Chad cried out, his voice filled with gut-wrenching anguish.

He was caught in the middle of a nightmare. Rachel stood there, a moment of decision plaguing her as she tried to decide what to do to help.

Chad moaned again, the sound more than Rachel could stand.

"Chad," she called out softly. "Chad, it's okay. You're okay," she crooned. Reaching out to touch his arm, she wanted to soothe away his nightmare. Calm him if such a thing were possible.

The second her hand connected, Chad's eyes flew open, his hand grabbing hers. "What are you doing," he asked, a combination of anguish and shock in his expression.

His steel-like grip held her in place.

"You were having a nightmare. I'm sorry. I only wanted to help."

Chad visibly forced himself to relax, letting out a deep breath and dropping her hand. "Okay, then."

"Do you want to talk about it?" she asked, keeping her voice low and soft.

He pulled back, his expression blank. "Hardly. It was a nightmare, and you're not my shrink," he said, his voice cold and distant, unlike the laughing, teasing man she'd spent time with the past few days.

"I was just trying to be nice, and it's no cause for rudeness. However, something is clearly bothering you, and if so, talking can be a good balm for the soul."

Chad shook his head. "If I need help, I'll ask. Right now, I'd like to be left alone so I can go back to sleep," he said, dismissing her.

Rachel could only guess the nightmare was related to his time in the military. If he refused to get help or talk to anyone, he'd never be free from a past that haunted him. She couldn't imagine all that he'd seen and done, her heartbreaking for the anguish he was suffering.

Patience.

It was as though God was trying to tell her something. Rachel vowed to be patient, but she might not have long enough to help, judging by Chad's reaction. The storm had passed, and already road crews were working on cleanup and clearing the roads. She turned and headed down the hall without so much as another word.

Chad might think she would let it go—but that's where he would be wrong. If she was unsuccessful in convincing him to seek help before she left, Rachel would do the one thing left she could do to help—call in backup. *Leslie.*

The rest of the night remained sleepless for Rachel, her brain in overdrive regarding Chad. But by the time breakfast rolled around, he had acted as though nothing had happened, although the undercurrents of tension rippled just beneath the exterior bravado he displayed. A bravado she hadn't been able to break through over the past two days with her attempts to lead him into a discussion.

They played games, ate meals together, and had even gone sledding again. Friends for sure, but confidants? *Not even close.*

The sun was shining brightly, warming the air with its radiant heat. Reports claimed the main roads were completely plowed and accessible, and it was only the back roads that remained problematic. Which meant it wouldn't be long before she'd be gone.

Rachel looked up as Chad came through the front door, looking tall, handsome, and completely worn out from all the shoveling he'd been doing since early this morning. "Making good progress?" she asked.

"I've made a path around the house, and the driveway is clear. Tomorrow, I will start a path down the gravel drive that leads back to the main road. Hopefully, by then, they will have the secondary roads all reopened for travel."

"Trying to get rid of me?" she teased.

Chad shrugged out of his jacket. "Cabin fever is more like it."

"If you say so. It's not like you wanted me here in the first place, so I reckon you'll be glad to see me leave." Rachel grinned. She didn't honestly believe it, but then with Chad, one never knew.

He moved to the living room and sat down next to the fire, holding out his hands for warmth. "I wouldn't go that far. You've been good company to have around when it comes to being snowed in."

Rachel was surprised he would admit such a thing. "Wow. What a nice compliment." Truth be told, she thought the same thing of him.

His gaze held hers, neither of them looking away. An awareness passed between them, like a silent message acknowledging their friendship. But it was more than that. A connection of sorts as if by getting through the past few days had been a test of wills, and they both came out winning—together. Well, all except the issue with Chad's nightmare.

"Have any luck with the applications you submitted for your next mission trip?" he asked, breaking the silence.

"Now I know you're trying to get rid of me," she teased.

"Just making conversation." Chad glanced at the Bible in her hands and turned back to the fire, but not before she saw the lines of tension crease his forehead.

Rachel figured now was as good a time as any to bring up the subject of the nightmare again. She'd prayed about what to do, and the helper gift God had given her wouldn't let her walk away without trying to reach Chad again. "I know this isn't a subject you want to discuss, but I can't help but feel we should. You can't shove what happened into the dark shadows, Chad. Do you think the nightmare is because you have a Post-Traumatic Stress Disorder?"

His gaze snapped to hers. "It's called PTSD, and I remember telling you to let it go. Why would you bring it up again?"

"Because I care about you. As a friend," she clarified, not wanting to send the wrong message. "Will you at least promise me you'll talk to someone?"

"No, little Miss Fix It, I won't promise anything. There's nothing that needs fixing," he said coldly.

So much for the easy friendship, but it had to be said. "Could have fooled me. You were afraid a bomb was going to explode. That's not a normal nighttime adventure, and considering your recent return from Afghanistan, it would make sense. Why would you be so stubborn about something you clearly need help with to move past and not let it haunt you?"

Chad let out a deep breath. "They're just flashbacks from the past. Given what I've seen, I'm not surprised. It's the same reason I want to help the kids. The horrors I've seen aren't a suitable conversation for a person who hasn't lived with them. Trust me."

She was surprised he'd given her this much information, and she decided to press forward, taking his admission as a sign. "We could pray together—for peace in your life. God can give you the strength to get through this and figure out how to move forward."

Chad shook his head and stood. "I'm not one of your mission projects, Rachel. Let it go. I stopped believing when I was deployed and came face to face with pure evil. Watching children die was more than I could bear."

"Those are people doing the killing. Not God. Men perpetrate evil. Those children are children of God, and that's who we're fighting for. We are fighting for common decency amongst one another as we are all equal and looking for a better future. But to understand that, you must have faith and the belief that God is ultimately in control."

"Save it for those who want to believe," Chad said, storming out of the room.

So much for the impasse. Rachel gazed out the window, watching as Chad picked up an ax and swung it with a vengeance, cutting firewood they didn't need. Every ounce of his fury landed with each strike.

Her heart ached for him. The best thing she could do to help him was to leave, giving him the space he needed. She moved to the front window, noting Chad's progress on clearing the driveway. Her vehicle wasn't that much farther down the road. All she had to do was dig the car out. Maybe she'd even be able to rock it back and forth and get free now that the snow was melting. It was a long shot, but one worth taking.

Spotting the shovel on the front porch, she came to a decision. Even if she couldn't back move the car, she'd be ready to go when the tow truck arrived. Maybe even catch a ride into town. Not to mention, it would help the snowplow see her vehicle as she didn't fancy them sideswiping the Audi.

Dressed warmly, Rachel headed out the front door. She eased down the path Chad had cleared, walking carefully to avoid slipping on the icy spots forming. Turning right at the end of the driveway, her way became much harder to navigate. The snow was quite deep but better than she could have hoped for. The trees had protected much of the road.

She gazed up at the sky as a vulture flew overhead, just in time for a heap of snow to land on her head as it melted off the tree branch. Brushing the cold snow out of her face, she shook her head, frustrated with Chad, the snowstorm, and her life. If he could see her now, she was sure he'd be laughing. Paybacks weren't fun.

Rachel spotted her car and quickened her pace. Little by little, she pushed the snow off the hood, the door handles, and the windows. That done, she started digging out around the vehicle, tossing the snow to the side of the road. Sweat beaded on her back, neck, and forehead. Shoveling had never been a favorite chore, and this was the worst. Pulling out the keys from her pocket, she unlocked the door and slid into the driver's seat.

She put the key in the ignition and turned it. Nothing happened. No lights. No sounds. Nothing. She tried again, with the same result. The battery was dead. Heaving a sigh of frustration, she got out of the car and relocked it. The trek back to the cabin would be a cold one, with the sweat cooling against her skin from the cold air temperature.

Off in the distance, a movement caught her attention. A big, black animal was meandering along the tree line of the woods.

Bear.

It was the first thing that came to mind. Rachel swallowed hard, adrenaline causing her heart to race in fear. She glanced back at the car, wondering if she should head that way and lock herself inside.

Or would he attack the vehicle with her in it? Unfortunately, she wasn't an expert on bear behavior. In fact, why he was even out made little sense. The bear should be hibernating based on everything she knew.

A low growl echoed in her direction, the bear altering his path to turn her way.

Decision made, Rachel ran for the car, terrified the bear intended to make her his lunch. Her hands shook as she tried to unlock the door, the keys dropping into the snow. She fell to her knees, swishing the snow around, trying to find them.

The bear was huffing as he pawed at the snow, still advancing.

Please, Lord, help protect me. When she left the cabin, an encounter with a bear was the last thing she'd expected.

So what was this bear's problem—besides her?

Chapter Eight

♥

L ATCHING ON TO HER keys, Rachel brushed off the snow sticking to the metal. Then, with another quick glance at the bear, she was relieved to see he had stopped advancing—at least for the moment. She tried to quell her shaking hand enough to push the key into the door lock, using both hands to steady her efforts.

Please, Lord, help me get this door open and to safety. As her fear escalated, her tension levels soared. Her throat was tight, and it was hard to breathe.

A shot rang out, the sound echoing down the wooded lane like thunder, causing her to jump. Another surge of adrenaline raced through her body as she spun around, intent on discovering the source. It was close. Off in the distance, she spotted someone running down the road from the direction of the cabin.

Chad.

Another shot rang out, and Rachel covered her ears. The bear hadn't liked the sound either and was now running into the woods. She let out a deep breath, the relief almost overwhelming. Partly because Chad had rescued her, and partly because she was grateful the bear wasn't his target. If Chad had planned to kill the bear, Mr. Military wouldn't have missed.

Rachel grabbed the shovel and headed toward him, meeting Chad halfway. "Thank you so much," she said, glancing down at his now holstered pistol. Rachel stepped in close to hug him, not even caring they had last parted in discord. When his arms came around her, she felt a second sense of relief.

"You're welcome," he drawled. "But I've got to ask, why are you even out here?"

Rachel pulled back. "Given the circumstances, I thought it would be best if I tried to dig out my car. Once the roads are cleared, I'll be leaving, and my vehicle was buried. But why are you out here? Not that I'm not grateful because I am forever in your debt. You probably saved my life."

Chad shrugged, a funny expression on his face. "I don't know if the bear would have attacked, but I didn't want to take any chances. He was probably looking for food, but not necessarily the human variety." He shot her a teasing smile, and it went a long way to unwinding her nerves.

"I thought bears hibernated in the winter," she said, still having a hard time understanding the animal's presence.

"Most do. You can't have spent much time in the mountains during the winter if you don't know our Smoky Mountain bears are different."

"Not really. There was always plenty to do in town without the bonus of bugs and roughing it in the woods." Not to mention her parents had busy social calendars that didn't allow for expeditions that didn't further their interests. And Alex had been more of a city fellow. Another reason she should have seen they weren't suited and been brave enough to put an end to the relationship before it had gone as far as it did.

Chad took the shovel from her. "When we have warm spells in the winter, they come looking for food. I reckon the storm drove them into their dens, and today's sunshine is warm and welcoming to an animal out scavenging around for a meal."

"Something I didn't know but won't forget." She grinned. "So why did you come looking for me? You didn't say." They started down the road toward the cabin, matching their steps to the existing footprints.

"I was looking for you in the cabin because I wanted to apologize for my earlier gruffness. But when I discovered you were gone, it was easy enough to figure out where you were headed after I spotted your footprints at the end of the driveway. I figured it would be good to follow and see what you were up to, and if I could help."

"Well, I'm glad you did." She reached out to touch his arm. "Thank you, Chad. Let's just call everything that's happened these past days even. Friends?" she asked, holding out her hand.

"Friends." He shook her hand. "Shall we?" He gestured toward the cabin. "Wouldn't want you catching a chill out here after all your hard work."

Rachel nodded. "I am cold. I think it's all the sweat freezing on my skin."

Chad took his scarf and wrapped it around her neck. "This and the walk back should help."

His concern was touching. "Thank you." Rachel had to agree with Leslie; her brother was a nice guy. More than that, he had a big heart, even if he tried to hide it from her.

An awkward silence fell between them.

"About earlier," Chad said, pausing to glance in her direction. "The whole PTSD thing. I really am sorry about the way I acted. It's just that I don't like to talk about it. It brings up a whole slew of negative memories that I'm trying to forget, not dredge up."

"I understand. I shouldn't have pressed you so hard. Sometimes my helper gift gets me into trouble," she said, regretting her part in their argument.

Chad stopped, turning to face her. "It wasn't personal, I promise. And I hope it's not why you're in an all-fire hurry to leave."

"Well, I did feel it would be best. It is your home, and I'm the unwelcome guest you're stuck with for the time being." They'd had their moments of fun, plenty of them. But that's all it was, and the reality was still present. The term *unwelcome guest* said it all.

They resumed walking. "I don't mind you being here. Honestly."

"That's good to know," Rachel said, knocking into his arm playfully, hoping to return to the easy camaraderie they'd share.

"The thing is...the community center is my focus, not the past. I told you about the kids I want to help at the center—but I didn't tell you why. In Afghanistan, children are used as weapons of war, and it's heartbreaking. It's the images I can't get out of my head, and sometimes they haunt me," Chad said, his voice vibrating with the same suffering she'd heard the night she witnessed his nightmare.

Rachel was honored that he trusted her with a glimpse into his private world—a world of pain and despair, and one she desperately hoped he found a way out of. He had so much to give the children. "Thank you for sharing something so personal. The program you're planning will be such a blessing to the children."

"That's what I'm hoping. Kids in need will have a free pass to join and build friendships with other kids who become members. Team building skills and life-building skills are at the top of the list. Anything that keeps a child moving forward in a positive direction." His voice had become vibrant with warmth and emotion, his passion for what he was doing obvious.

Chad's determination to forge ahead would stand up against any issues along the way, and Rachel was positive he would be successful with the program. "You've really thought this through, and it sounds wonderful. Kids from all over the country can come in for camp experiences. Have you thought about setting up a donation site? Extra funding can help pay to fly the kids here, and I'm sure people would love to get involved and help out financially."

"I hadn't gotten that far in my planning, but what a great idea." Chad opened the front door, holding it wide for her to enter.

The warmth of the fire was even better as she shrugged out of her coat and boots and moved to stand beside it, holding out her hands. "This feels so good. I'm starting to feel my fingers again."

"Hold that thought, and I'll be right back." Chad headed for the kitchen.

Alone, Rachel had time to ponder Chad's admission. PTSD was a serious matter, and it wouldn't go away on its own. She also knew better than to press him again, realizing Leslie was the better person to help her brother. Somethings were better left in the family.

Chad returned with a cup of hot chocolate, handing her one. "Here you go."

"Thank you," she said, taking a sip. "*Hmmm*. This is delicious."

"You're welcome." He took a seat on the sofa. "An idea occurred to me, and if you've got a few minutes, I'd love to run it by you."

Rachel moved to sit at the other end of the sofa, facing him. "Let's hear it."

"So, the thing is, you've mentioned how you like helping people."

"Yes, that's true. Too much sometimes, I fear." She grinned, knowing they both knew exactly what she was referring to.

Chad smiled, relaxing against the back cushion and getting comfortable. "Help is help, and I'm sure you have the best of intentions. The thing is, you seem completely on board with what I'm doing at the community center. I loved your inspired suggestion about funding and making this a national program. You're not working anywhere I know of, and I wondered if you would want to work for me—as the program manager at the community center. I'm hiring, and I need someone passionate about helping others and who's creative. I think you'd be awesome for the job given your experience in the mission field, your big heart, and your compassionate nature."

Rachel hadn't expected this and was unsure how to answer. It really was a great offer, and it would be something she would truly enjoy under different circumstances. The timing was all wrong. "I consider it an honor you even thought of me for the position, but I'm sorry. I don't think it's a good idea."

"Because of me?" he asked, a frown etched across his face.

She shook her head, not wanting him to get the wrong impression. "No, because of me. I just got out of a relationship, and I have the freedom to do what I want—which I've already explained was to travel on mission trips. I don't want to be tied down, and a job would do just that—tie me down."

"I see." His tone said otherwise.

"Like I told you already, I've been applying to several mission projects, and I'm hoping to hear back soon. It's my dream to travel and follow my heart wherever it leads me, wherever God calls me to go. And the last thing I want is someone looking over my shoulder, telling me what to do, how I should act, or anything else. I've had enough of that with my parents over the years, and even Alex to some degree."

"Well, okay then. I guess that's that. Consider the subject closed. Are you up for a game of backgammon before dinner?" Chad was quick to change the subject, recognizing her refusal was genuine and not personal.

"Sure. I don't mind a chance to beat you again," she teased, trying to lighten the mood.

"Wishful thinking," Chad retorted.

Wishful thinking was wishing she could be in two places at once—*the mission field and helping Chad because a part of her wanted to stay and see where their friendship would lead.*

Chapter Nine

♥

RACHEL'S PHONE RANG AS she unplugged it from the charger. The ringtone announced it was her mother calling. She knew it was time to talk to her, but still, Rachel hesitated. Over the past couple of days, her parents had called often. Each time she texted them back, letting them know she was okay. But, unfortunately, the calls were growing more frequent, and it was time to face the parental music.

Even if she was twenty-five.

She pressed the accept button. "Hey, Mom. What's up?" she asked, aiming for a light and cheery tone.

"It's about time you answered the phone, young lady. If it weren't for the storm, I would have been at that cabin days ago to talk you out of this nonsense." Her mother was in rare form, ready to bulldoze her daughter in the direction she saw fit.

Too bad they weren't on the same page because it would be wonderful to have an advocate of her caliber. But pitted against Rachel, she was a formidable opponent. "It's not nonsense. It's peaceful here and exactly what I needed. There's a difference," Rachel insisted.

Knock. Knock.

Rachel stood and headed toward the cracked-open door, intent on signaling Chad to remain quiet. Conveniently, she had failed to mention Chad in the texts she'd sent her mother.

He pushed the door open a little further before she could get there. "Good morning, Rachel. Are you decent?" Chad asked, a teasing grin on his face. He knew the door would be shut tight and locked if she weren't decent.

She pointed to the phone and covered the speaker, hoping he'd get the message.

"I just wanted to let you know I'll be out back chopping more wood, and then we can fix breakfast if that's okay with you?"

"Rachel Lyn, who's that man I hear in the background," her mother demanded.

So much for the secret warning not to speak. Rachel pulled the door open wide. This time, she held a finger up to her lips, nodding her understanding of what he said, and again, vigorously pointed at the phone.

Chad nodded, turned, and left—much to her relief.

"Rachel, I asked you a question. Is that Alex? Why is he there with you? And how did he get there? The back roads aren't passable yet, at least not that I know of. And I saw him with your wedding planner yesterday. Alex is still talking to her about the wedding. Did you know about that? He knows he made a mistake, and it was a simple case of cold feet. But I reckon if he's with you now, you know all this. I'm glad the two of you are working things out."

Rachel held the phone away from her ear. Her mother went on and on about Alex, and it was giving her a tension headache. "Mom, stop." Rachel knew why Alex was talking to the wedding planner, but she wasn't at liberty to enlighten her mother. "Alex isn't here, and we aren't getting back together." She rubbed her forehead and waited for the backlash.

"But the two of you are perfect together. This is all a misunderstanding. Come back and talk to Alex.

We still have the wedding decorations, and we can simply move forward and get this done. You know this is what's best for you."

That's just it...it wasn't what was best—for either one of them. "You're not listening. I'm not going to marry Alex, and he doesn't want to marry me. We've talked, and we're both okay on that score. I don't think I ever really wanted to marry him. It just seemed like the logical next step. It was what you and Dad wanted, not us. And then, with his parents pressuring us to get married, we simply went along. I don't love him the way a woman should love her husband." Rachel let out a deep sigh, hoping her mother would finally accept the truth.

"Those things take time. You don't know what you're saying. And if that's not Alex there with you, who is it?"

Rachel knew her mother would circle back to the issue. "It's Chad McCarthy. Leslie's brother."

"I thought he was in Afghanistan. Why is he with you?" she asked, her voice suddenly tight and shrill.

"Chad was deployed. Now he's not. And Chad's here because he owns the place, and when he returned home, this is where he decided to stay. I'm here because I didn't know Chad was here, and I got snowed in. It's no big deal," Rachel said, trying to explain, but knowing all the while, the truth wouldn't sit well with her mother. It never did when it came to her daughter.

"Of course, it's a big deal. It's not right you are there alone with a man. What will the people in town say, for heaven's sake? And what will Alex say? You two will never work things out if he thinks you've been shacking up with some other guy. Honestly, Rachel, you have got yourself into a bad situation. That's what comes from overreacting and running off like you did after Alex jilted you at the altar. I gave him a piece of my mind for that inappropriate behavior."

Rachel closed her eyes and rubbed at her forehead. "Gee, thanks for the reminder, Mom. I left so I wouldn't have to listen to people talk about it in front of me like I wasn't there. The same way you're doing now. And I can't help what people say about Chad and me being here together as it was an act of Mother Nature, not some clandestine affair we planned out. And as to Alex, I don't care what he thinks." Not to mention, Mother Nature was under

God's control, so, therefore, it could be reasoned that perhaps she had been stranded here for a reason. *And the reason was to help Chad.* Something she hadn't thought of before with everything going on.

"I'm coming there as soon as the roads open and will stay with you until you're ready to come home. You're clearly distraught over this whole situation. Or maybe you should think about coming home when the roads are passable instead of making me go stay there. It's much more comfortable at our house than that little cabin of theirs would be. I'm sure of it."

Rachel thought differently. The cabin was cozy and filled with warmth. "My car slid in the ditch. As soon as I can get a tow truck here, I'll come home. But I'm not staying in town long. I've sent out several applications, and I'm trying to get assigned to another mission trip."

"But you just got home, dear. I'll come to get you, so don't worry. You can hold off leaving and give Alex another chance to make things right."

Nothing ever seemed to change. "Mom, do you hear yourself? You aren't listening to a thing I've said. There will be no wedding. And I'm old enough to do what I want with my life, which includes leaving again on a mission trip." Why she felt the need to defend her actions was beyond Rachel, but her mother always seemed to make her feel like a little kid again.

"I'm listening. I just don't like what I'm hearing. I'll find a way to come get you, dear. Then we can sit and have a cozy little talk. You're simply stressed out right now and shouldn't make decisions that will affect your future."

"No, Mom. Don't come here. Alex and I aren't together anymore. And Chad and I are friends, that's it. End of story. And I'll call Leslie to come to get me as soon as the roads are safe. I know she wants to see her brother." Rachel was grasping at straws to keep her mother away. Maybe she could even stay with Leslie for a few days. That would certainly go a long to easing the perpetual headache she would have at home listening to her mother drone on about Alex and her.

"Fine. But if Leslie can't get there, you let me know. Your father will be worried sick when I tell him you're up there with a man. Leslie's brother or otherwise, he's still single."

It was like living in the dark ages. "Yes, Mother. I understand." *It was also easier to agree.*

On a more positive note, at least Chad hadn't heard her mother's comments. That would have been the ultimate humiliation. Twenty-five years old and her own mother didn't trust her to make the right decisions. Having been brought up attending church every Sunday, it's not like she didn't know the rules. The Bible was clear on a lot of things, but not once had she ever read, thou shall not cohabitate with a man in a snowstorm, and that instead, you should freeze out in the cold.

Rachel headed down the hall, checking to make sure Chad was still outside. Spotting him at the woodpile, she watched the way he swung the ax, driving it into the log and splitting the wood apart with a force that spoke of his strength. She hit the speed dial button for Leslie, wanting to get the call over with before Chad came inside.

"Hey, Rachel. We must be in harmony as I was just about to call and see how you were doing," Leslie said, her cheery voice a welcome relief after talking to her mother.

"Maybe so. I'm doing well, given the circumstances. Your brother is sweet and fun to be around, most of the time anyway." Rachel chuckled.

"I warned you to keep a close eye on him."

"You did at that, but he hasn't tried to pull any practical jokes yet, so it's all good. In fact, he saved me from a bear. So I'd say he's a pretty handy guy to have around," Rachel said, trying to figure out a way to ease into the reason for her call.

"What are you talking about? Did a bear try to attack you? Are you okay?" Leslie asked.

"Slow down. A bear came around looking for food. I'm just not sure if I was on the menu. Chad showed up and wasn't about to give the bear time to decide. He ran him off with a couple of gunshots in the air. I was scared, but it's all good now."

"Thank goodness. I bet that was scary."

"It was, but everything is good now. I promise. Listen, I've got a few things I wanted to discuss. As soon as I get an assignment on a mission trip, I'll be leaving again. There's something I need to tell you about your brother before that happens. Something important, but not something he'd want me to mention...but the thing is...I can't *not* tell you."

"For goodness sake, just spit it out. Has he done something wrong? Do I need to kill my brother?" Leslie asked, a touch of teasing in her voice. She knew her brother better than to think there was any real problem.

"Chad's suffering from PTSD, and he does not want to tell anyone about it." It almost felt as though she were betraying his confidence, but *not* to tell would leave him to fend for himself. And few soldiers ever got through something like this on their own.

"Oh no. What happened? Tell me everything you know." Leslie's voice had grown tense.

"I don't want to say too much as it's his life and the events are personal. I just thought you should know so that after I leave, you can keep an eye on him, maybe even persuade him to seek help." Rachel was walking a fine line on how much to tell. She prayed this was the right thing to do.

"You have to give me more to go on," Leslie said, pressing for more information.

"The thing is, Chad saw some terrible things while deployed, and he has nightmares. He's planning on opening a community center to help children who have lost a parent in war. It's quite admirable, but I would hate to see him self-destruct on the inside and then lose touch with everything else on the outside. Everyone loses if that happens. Anything more than this, and you'll need to find a way to ask him yourself."

"I appreciate your willingness to protect Chad's privacy, and I'm glad you told me. He can be stubborn, but I can be too. I promise I'll keep an eye on him."

Rachel was relieved, knowing her friend would follow through. "Thank you. I'll feel better when I'm gone knowing he won't slip through the cracks. Not with you watching over him." Chad might not appreciate her getting involved, but the weight of knowing and not sharing was a heavy burden to bear. It was for his own good, even if he didn't see it that way.

"Okay, thanks. I'm still upset with Chad that he came home and didn't bother to tell me."

It was all part of Chad's issues, something Rachel fully understood now. "I think he wanted time and space to try and work out some of those issues I mentioned."

"Are you defending him?" Leslie asked, curiosity lacing her voice.

Maybe. Probably. "Not at all. There's nothing to defend. It's your family cabin, and he came home. End of story."

"*Hmmm.* Interesting." Leslie's brain had gone into overdrive, and Rachel needed a change in subject.

"Not really." They were two people, forced to cohabitate, and who had become friends. Nothing else. But then there was the almost kiss.

"So you said three reasons. What are the others?"

"I almost hate to ask, but as soon as the back roads are cleared and open, do you think you could come to get me? I'm hoping it will be done as early as tomorrow. And I'm also hoping you'll let me come stay with you for a few days." The cabin was lovely, and her time here with Chad would always be memorable, but this wasn't reality. Just an escape from reality when she needed it most.

"Of course you can stay with me. But what's your hurry to leave? You haven't even been there a week."

"My mother. She's having a cow. She has even threatened to come and chaperone me here until I leave, or preferably take me home. She thinks

I'm distraught and need someone to lend a guiding hand."

"Sounds just like your mother." Leslie chuckled. "I'm sure that was a fun conversation."

"According to her, Alex and I belong together, and I should give him a second chance. And I'm ruining my chances for a reconciliation being up here in the cabin alone with Chad."

"What? Give me a break. It's called snowed-in. And as to Alex, no way. That was a lucky escape on your part. Speaking of, he's been seen around town and quite cozy with your wedding planner. I don't think he's trying to keep it a secret anymore."

"Alex's family, and my own for that matter, think those two are still planning my wedding with Alex, not their own. He's waiting to break it to his parents when everything quiets down."

"Wow. They are in for a rude awakening."

Total understatement. "Agreed."

"So, what do you think of my brother?" Leslie asked, returning to the part of the conversation Rachel thought she'd safely avoided.

"What do I think of your brother as what?" This wasn't a conversation she wanted to have with

Leslie seeing as she was Chad's sister. Talk about awkward.

"You know...like as in your next special someone."

This was exactly what she feared, mainly because the truth was, she did like Chad. More than she should, considering she wasn't sticking around the area and there was no place for anything more between them. Not to mention, Chad had his own ideas about the future. "Leslie...stop. I'm not looking to jump into a relationship a week after my miserable wedding day."

"It wasn't your wedding day, seeing as you didn't get married. I like to think of it as your freedom day," Leslie teased.

"Exactly. So why would I want to be tied down to anyone? And as to your brother, that would be plain weird. Luckily, he doesn't seem to be on the lookout for a girlfriend either. I think Chad and I will stick to friends—thank you very much."

"*Hmmm.* And I think you protest too much."

There it was again...her friend was overthinking the situation. "Chad's a nice guy, but we are not on the same page. I'm looking to travel, and he's looking to settle down in one place. We are complete opposites."

"They say opposites attract," Leslie said, pushing back and trying to poke holes in Rachel's practical view.

It was time to change the subject as she wasn't sure Leslie would give up easily. "Are you going to come to get me when the roads are cleared, or not? Please don't make me have to ask my mother."

"Of course, I will. In fact, if you want, I'll fire up the snowmobile in the morning and head that way. Won't need to wait for the roads to be cleared."

"Wait…what? I thought the sled was in the shop getting fixed. Otherwise, I might have asked you sooner."

"It was, and now it's not," Leslie said, her matter-of-fact tone glossing over the implications of her words.

"So you could have come to get me after the storm let up?" Rachel shook her head. The least her friend could have done was offer to pick her up, but clearly, Leslie had an ulterior motive. Pushing her and Chad together once she found out he was in residence at the cabin.

"Not really. I needed the road crews to clear the secondary roads to get close enough to trailer the sled in. There's a parking lot over about fifteen miles from the cabin where I can unload and then make my way through the woods to get to you."

"I see. Then I guess you are off the hook. Otherwise, I would have thought you left me here with your brother on purpose."

"If I had, could you blame me?" Leslie laughed. "It would be nice to officially become sisters."

"I already consider you my sister, so I don't need to marry your brother for that to become a reality. Goodbye, Leslie," Rachel said, hitting the disconnect button.

Chad was done splitting wood and had a nice, neat stack by the back door, ready to haul inside. Cold air blasted into the room as he entered, stomping the snow off his boots on the mat. His cheeks were rosy and red as he smiled, snatching off his black beanie. "I've worked up a hunger. Any chance you fixed breakfast? I can bring the wood in later." He peered around her, glancing into the kitchen, a hopeful expression on his face.

Rachel shook her head. "Sorry, no such luck. But I can warm us up some waffles. Or even cook the box of blueberry muffins...if you trust me, that is," she teased.

"Waffles sound good. And they're easy since they cook in the toaster. We could go all out and put strawberry jelly on them. I remember doing that as a kid."

"Coming right up." Rachel headed for the kitchen, leaving Chad to get washed. She popped the waffles in the toaster, warmed the jelly, and poured Chad a cup of coffee. Grabbing an orange, she peeled and sectioned it, placing the pieces on the edge of his plate. Putting everything on a tray, Rachel headed for the dining table just as Chad returned.

"Looks like good timing," he said, pulling out a seat. "Wow, this looks nice. And nothing is burned—even better."

"That was only the first time we cooked, and it was a joint effort if I remember correctly." Rachel enjoyed the back-and-forth teasing, and cooking was one easy subject to joke about.

"Maybe." He shrugged, taking a seat. After stuffing a few bites of waffle in his mouth, he washed it down with coffee. "This is good, but then I'm hungry."

"Thanks a lot. I was trying to be helpful and show my appreciation for all that you've done to make this past week easy for us."

"You are helpful. You can peel my orange anytime." Chad grinned as he shot her a wink.

"Ha-ha." Rachel continued to eat her breakfast, unsure how to tell him about Leslie's imminent arrival. It was the end to her time at the cabin, but also an end to Chad's privacy.

"Who were you talking to earlier?" he asked.

"My mom." It was the opening she needed. "She was going to find a way to get here tomorrow and chaperone us if I planned on staying here any longer. You'd think I was a baby or something." Rachel scrunched up her face in distaste.

"You'll always be her baby. Moms tend to worry."

Rachel let out a heavy sigh. "Well, mine worries too much and thinks she knows best for my whole life."

"Ouch. That would be a serious issue." Chad reached for the syrup and poured more onto his waffle.

"Tell me about it."

"That would be a serious issue," Chad repeated.

Rachel frowned. "Yes, you said that."

"You said—"

"I get it. Ha-ha. Leslie said you're a jokester." Better Chad have his fun with wordplay than having him put peanut butter in her hair or whatever else the man could dream up.

"You talked to her also?" Chad asked, his brow lines deepening as the easy grin disappeared.

"Yes, but not about the jokester thing. That was the first day I got here when I was checking up on you, I might add."

"So what was today about then?" he asked, his gaze intent on her.

"I've asked her to come to get me tomorrow morning. She's trailering the snowmobile to the parking lot about fifteen miles away and then headed here. My car needs a tow truck, and I need to get back to town, and with the threat of my mother's arrival, I decided Leslie was a much better choice."

"My sister is coming here?"

"Yes. Is that a problem?" Rachel said, rising to take her plate to the sink and rinse it off.

"The reason I didn't tell her I was coming home was to have some privacy. Now, she'll be camping out underfoot and asking hundreds of questions." Chad had grown distant, the wall between them higher than ever.

His sister was bound to come eventually, so what was the big deal. "I'm sorry."

"You didn't happen to mention my little problem, did you?"

So that's what he was worried about. Rachel felt her face flush red with the truth, but she wasn't going to admit a thing to Chad. "It's not a little problem. Look at the bright side. With me gone, you can have the place to yourself. At least one of your problems will be solved."

"There is that."

Rachel was glad he hadn't pressed her for more information as she would have had to tell him the truth. *Lord, please forgive me, but you know I told Leslie to help him. I just don't think Chad would appreciate the interference for the love it was given in.*

Chapter Ten

♥

B REAKFAST WASN'T THE MOST social of affairs. Chad had become distant, but Rachel couldn't tell if it was because his sister was due to arrive this morning or if he was nervous as to what she might have told her best friend. Or maybe he was still put out because she'd said no to his job offer.

Whatever it was didn't matter because it all added up to a gulf between them that hadn't existed since he first discovered her in the cabin. Lucky for Rachel, she was leaving, and soon this would become just another memory.

A good one for the most part. Chad could be charming, fun, considerate, had a huge heart for kids. Of course, there was his inability to cook and his occasional moodiness. The cooking problem was one they shared. And as to his moodiness, Chad was entitled to the condition more than most. He'd been through a lot recently.

With the dishes finished, Rachel headed to the bedroom. Pulling out her suitcase, she repacked her clothes and shoes. Most of it hadn't been worn, considering they were sunny, honeymoon outfits. She snapped the locks closed and wheeled it down the hall, expecting any minute to hear a snowmobile approaching.

The weather was warmer today with the full sun beating down. There was still no sign of Chad, and Rachel headed out to the porch to wait for her friend.

She settled into one of the comfortably padded rocking chairs, enjoying the crisp, cool air and the sound of the birds calling out to one another. A male cardinal landed on an evergreen tree nearby, his bright red color against the snow-covered green branches picture perfect. She pulled out her phone and snapped a few photos, trying to capture the magic of the moment.

Leslie's ring tone blasted into the peaceful silence, startling the cardinal, and he flew away. "Hey there. Where are you? I thought you'd be here by now, considering when you left," Rachel said, eager to see her friend again.

"Change of plans," Leslie said, her voice laced with tension.

"Why? What's wrong?" Rachel asked, a knot forming in her stomach.

"Promise you won't freak out or anything. I'm doing enough of that on my own."

"What is it? What's wrong?" Rachel asked again, her stomach twisting in a multitude of knots now.

"There was an accident. I don't remember much, but the guy came around a curve too fast, and I tried to avoid him. What happened after that is kind of vague, but I'm in the hospital. I'm sorry, but I won't be coming to get you anytime today."

"But are you okay? I mean, why are you in the hospital? Is it serious?" Rachel's brain was racing with all the possible scenarios but tried to remain calm. Leslie was talking to her, which was a good sign.

"Broken arm. Possible concussion. Bruises. That sort of thing. The doctor wants to keep me here overnight to monitor my condition and watch for any signs of trauma to the head."

"Oh, my goodness. I'm so sorry. What else did the doctor say?" Rachel felt awful as a sick feeling of dread washed over her. This was her fault. If she hadn't asked Leslie to come to get her, this wouldn't have happened.

"Not much. I blacked out, so the doctors aren't taking any chances. They've ordered a CT scan. That's all I know."

"Does Chad know?" Rachel asked, the twisting knot in her stomach doubling in size.

"What do you mean? Aren't you with him? And no, I wanted to tell you and let you be the one to tell him. He'd freak out on the phone with me, and I really don't need more stress at the moment." Leslie knew her brother all too well and was right.

Rachel closed her eyes, the thought of being the bearer of bad news, not a job she wanted. "I see. And yes, he's here, but he's avoiding me."

"Why?" Leslie asked, the single-word question direct and to the point.

One she couldn't ignore. "Because I asked you to come to get me. Chad's worried I told you about the PTSD and that you're coming here to rescue him."

"You did tell me. So what's the big deal?"

"He's a private person, and like I said, he didn't want anyone to know about it. The fact I do has strained our friendship, more so, now that he thinks I've brought you in on it."

"Chad's my brother, and I know all about how closed off he can be, but if there's one thing I learned over the years, it's how to handle him. Or at least I will be able to after you calm him down about the accident. Just reassure him everything will be okay. Please, Rachel. He can be a bit protective of me at times."

She wouldn't deny her friend anything, especially as she was lying in a hospital bed and it was all Rachel's fault. "I'll tell him. You have my word. I'm so sorry I asked you to come to get me. I should have just waited...but my mom. I shouldn't have let her get to me. This is terrible."

"A broken arm is inconvenient. A broken head would be a bigger concern. But God was watching over me, and I'll be all right. You're like a sister to me, and I'd do anything for you. Sometimes, things happen outside of our control, but we can't stop living because something bad might happen. If we did that, we miss all the good in life as well."

Leslie was right, of course, but it didn't make the guilt for her part in what happened to lighten even a smidgeon. "I hear you. I'm going to try and find another way to get to town so I can come and see you."

"Rachel, you don't have to. I'm sure everything will be fine. You just take care of my brother. Trust me. That can be a full-time job."

"Humor me. I want to be with you. We can help each other like we always have." Rachel would go whether Leslie agreed or not, even if it meant calling her mother. Some things were far more critical, and Leslie was one of them.

"Okay. I could use a ride home tomorrow if the doctor releases me. They said my car had to be towed and wasn't drivable. And at this point, I have no idea what happened to the snowmobile."

"I'll break the news to Chad. Hopefully, he's got some ideas who will come out this way to give me a ride into town. And I bet he can make some calls to figure out what's going on. You just concentrate on getting better and out of the hospital." Rachel hadn't stopped pacing the floor, but she drew up short when she spotted Chad walking out to the shed.

"We have a caretaker for the property. Ask Chad for his number. I'm sure the guy will help you, given the circumstances. I've got to hang up; the doctor just came in."

"Okay. Love you, girl."

"You too," Leslie said before the line went dead.

Thank you, Lord, for keeping her safe. Please forgive me for asking her to come to my aid. I should have stood up to my mother, but I try to be respectful. Unfortunately, it's getting me nowhere.

Rachel headed down the hall and grabbed her jacket. With each step she took toward the shed, her heart grew heavier, worried about Chad's reaction. He was hammering a couple of nails into the siding and oblivious to her approach. "Chad," she called out, alerting him to her presence.

He looked up and let out a heavy sigh. "I guess this means my sister is here, and you're leaving?" he asked, glancing toward the cabin.

"No, and yes, in that order." The decisive moment was upon her.

"What do you mean?" Chad slid the hammer into the tool belt around his waist and turned his full attention to her.

She put her hands together and twisted them, trying to quell her nerves. "Don't freak out, but Leslie's in the hospital. She's okay, or mostly okay."

Chad jerked back, taking in her words. "Tell me what you know," he ordered, his brisk tone authoritative and commanding.

"Sh...she was in an accident on the w...w...way here. I'm sorry, it's all my fault." This was even harder than she'd imagined.

"I don't think whose fault is of concern at the moment. Far more important is the matter of how Leslie is doing." He pulled out his phone.

"You can't call her right now. The doctor is with her. Leslie has a broken arm and is under concussion protocol. They're keeping her overnight for observation since she blacked out and doesn't remember anything after the other vehicle came into her lane and hit her." Rachel forced herself to repeat everything she knew, trying to relay all the details in hopes of calming Chad down a bit.

"Why didn't she call me?" he snapped.

"Honestly, she didn't want to deal with this…your reaction, that is."

"How else am I supposed to react? My sister is in the hospital and needs me, and I'm stuck on the mountain with the selfish woman who couldn't sit still another day. Leslie had no business driving on the back roads that aren't fully cleared yet."

So much for not worrying about who was at fault just yet, as it would seem he'd already come to his own conclusion. "You're right, and I'm sorry." There was no defense she could give that would make any sense.

Chad rubbed his forehead and then the back of his neck, lines of tension rippling across his forehead. "I've got to get to the hospital. Leslie's all I've got," he said, his voice almost breaking.

"She mentioned the caretaker. So I told Leslie I would come into town, and she thought you could set it up for him to come to get me."

"You?" he said, derision lacing his voice. "I'm Leslie's brother. If Charles comes here, it'll be me going into town to make sure she's okay. You've done enough."

"I get it, but it doesn't change anything. I need to leave, and I'm going to see my best friend whether you like it or not. So please, get two rides off this mountain. Remember, she called me first." Rachel needed to see her friend if only to make sure Leslie would be okay. Anything to make the gut-wrenching ache in her stomach disappear.

Chad paled; his expression one of torment. He had seen awful events in his life, and this was sure to rattle him. His comments and reaction were based on the fear of something happening to his sister. And he hadn't been able to protect her any more than he'd been able to protect the children in a country torn by war.

Rachel had gone too far with her comment. Her heart ached for the man standing in front of her, a deep pain reflected in his eyes. "I'm sorry, I shouldn't have said that. We both need and want to see her. Hopefully, you can make it happen. Until then, I'll be in the cabin." Rachel turned and walked away, unwilling to say anything else. Guilt was eating at her, and Chad's comments only made it worse—because he was right.

Rachel warmed her hands by the fire, praying the doctors didn't find anything else wrong with Leslie. Not five minutes later, she heard the back door slam shut.

Chad entered the room. "Charles has two guys coming in on snowmobiles to take us into town. So be ready in one hour. And for the record, I talked to Leslie, and there have been no updates, but it was good to hear her voice." The relief was evident in his demeanor.

The cabin should have been a peaceful retreat after the wedding disaster. But, instead, it had turned out to be another disaster. One to add to a long and clearly, still growing list of poor choices Rachel kept making in her life.

Chapter Eleven

♥

THE SNOWMOBILE TRANSPORT HAD been nothing short of a wild ride, one Rachel was relieved when it was over and they arrived at the caretaker's home. Maybe if she had been the one driving, it would have been more fun. But, instead, she'd hung on for dear life as they raced through the woods and back to the edge of civilization.

Charles had been kind enough to loan Chad his truck, and the long ride back to Edgewood was nothing of a test of wills as they searched for small talk and failed for the most part.

He turned into the hospital visitor parking lot and drove each row, searching for a spot and pulling in when he found one. Side by side, his pace nothing short of a brisk walk, borderline run, they entered the big double sliding-glass doors. Chad moved to the front reception desk, leaving her to follow.

"Excuse me, my name is Chad McCarthy, and I'm looking to find my sister's room. Leslie McCarthy. She was in an accident this morning, and they are keeping her overnight," he said, his voice rippling with tension.

The nurse smiled at him. "I'm not so old I don't remember you, young man. Or you, Rachel Harrelson. Been in this small town too long, not to know." She grinned. "Your sister is on the second floor. She's doing fine last I heard.' The woman glanced down at her clipboard. "Room 222. Down the hall to the elevator, right turn when you exit."

"Thank you, Mary. You always did have a great memory as the school nurse," Rachel said, helping Chad out as he tried to place the woman.

Mary beamed, pleased Rachel had remembered. "Run along, you two. I'm sure Leslie will be glad to have visitors," she said, shooing them away.

Chad shot Rachel a grateful look, but one that quickly disappeared. "Okay, and thanks for the information." He headed down the hall, leaving Rachel to follow once again.

"Can we please put aside our differences for the moment? I'm not sure it will help Leslie," Rachel said, leveling him with a confidence she was far from feeling.

He turned to her and shrugged. "Sure thing. I've just got a lot on my mind. It's not all you, trust me."

Not all her still meant partly her, but at least it offered her a little more reassurance.

Chad stepped back, allowing her to enter the room ahead of him. And given the fact he was Leslie's brother, it was a kind gesture that spoke volumes.

Leslie glanced their way, a gentle smile lighting her face when she recognized her visitors. "Hey, you two. I never thought you'd be able to get here today. What a great surprise."

"Of course, we're here." Rachel leaned down to kiss her friend's forehead. "I'm just so sorry this happened."

"Stop. I keep telling you it's not your fault. The other driver wasn't respecting the road conditions, and the blame lands squarely on his shoulders."

Rachel glanced at Chad, hoping that some of this conversation was sinking in. It was bad enough she was beating herself up over the situation, without him laying it on thicker.

"Any updates on your condition? I can't believe you wouldn't call and tell me yourself," Chad said, standing next to the bed, sizing Leslie up as if to reassure himself she was truly okay.

"And I can't believe you didn't tell me you left the army and were back home. Makes us even, don't you think?" Leslie countered.

"Guess your brain isn't rattled as much as they think, 'cause you're still sharp as a tack with the comebacks. Some things never change," Chad said, ruffling Leslie's hair.

"And some things do," Leslie said, leveling him with a matter-of-fact look. "The CT scan came back clear. So now it's just a standard concussion protocol, and they will keep me overnight. So relax. Besides, with no car and only one good arm, I'll get better food service than I could at home." Leslie laughed.

"Clearly, you've not eaten hospital food any time recently." Chad scrunched up his face in distaste and shook his head.

"True. Maybe you could sneak me in some fried chicken and some macaroni and cheese. I can just taste it already. Pleasssseee," Leslie whined, turning on her irresistible smile.

"I'll see what I can do." Chad shot his sister a smile and winked. "Now that I've seen you for myself, and you have a good report, why don't I let the two of you talk. I've got some important calls to make."

Leslie nodded. "Good, because I need to talk to Rachel about a few things."

Chad left the room, and Rachel pulled up a chair, needing to be closer to Leslie.

Seeing her did help—a lot. Other than the cast on her arm, her friend appeared to be doing well. "What can I get you? Do you need a drink? Or need the nurse for anything?" Rachel asked.

"I'm well cared for, so stop worrying. Now tell me, what's going on with you and my brother?" Leslie made a deep dive into the one subject Rachel wasn't prepared to discuss.

"Nothing. I told you that. You need to get Chad talking about the community center. It's a great plan and the perfect way to help so many children who have lost a parent and need a mentor. His vision is amazing and will be a true blessing to the community."

Leslie eyed her more closely. "Sounds to me like Chad has made quite an impression on you. Sweet." She grinned. "As to the community center, I love the idea. I also never knew my brother was a kid person, so that's an interesting but nice change."

"The war changed a lot of things for him, I think. Don't forget your promise to talk to him. After I'm gone," she emphasized.

Leslie nodded and took a sip of water. "I will. But it's not like you aren't coming back. Have you heard from any of the mission organizations yet?"

"Some, but there wasn't any vacancy on the teams. I've sent out a few more. Even one to the Alaskan Outreach Center. It's always been my dream to go there, and they needed someone to help in the classrooms with the younger kids. It would be an amazing opportunity." The first time she'd ever landed on the website, she'd felt a rush of adrenaline. Alaska. The last frontier. A place where wildlife photos and landscapes would abound. It was one of the most demanded programs to get into, seeing as every other volunteer dreamed of going to Alaska.

"Sounds it. But I still wish you didn't have to leave again so soon. If you stayed, maybe Chad and you—"

"Stop with the matchmaking. I'm not even close to ready for a relationship, and you, of all people, should know it." Leslie wanted her to be happy, but she needed to understand that her happiness didn't have to be attached to a man. Instead, she was ready to take charge of her life and make her own happiness.

"Can't blame me for trying. It would be perfect. Just think of all the fun we could have, and the holidays. Oh, they would be such a joy."

"Maybe so, but not my kind of perfect," Rachel teased. "An overbearing guy who wants to be in control. No, thank you. And to pull off this community service project—he's totally committed and in control."

A nurse came into the room. "How are you feeling, Leslie?"

Leslie shrugged. "I'm good. A little tired, though."

"That's normal. Your body has been through a lot, and it's trying to fight back in the best way it knows how. Get some rest. I'll give you a little sedative, and you can settle in for a good nap."

She shot Rachel an apologetic look. "Okay. I'm sorry, Rachel. I know you just got here, but I'm so sleepy."

"It's all good. I'll catch a ride to my house and come by to see you later." Rachel leaned down and gave her friend a half hug, not wanting to hurt her.

Leslie stifled a yawn.

Rachel went in search of Chad to let him know his sister wanted to sleep. She entered the waiting room, spotting him off to the side and on his phone. Sitting down, she opted to wait for him to finish the call.

"We make a good team, Andrea. I want you. Trust me, I'll give you as much freedom as you need. I would never want to hold you back from whatever it is you want to accomplish, especially if it benefits me."

Andrea? Chad was practically proposing to the woman on the phone—not a grand romantic gesture by any means.

It was the first she heard of the woman, not that she knew all the personal details of Chad's life. A seed of jealousy was planted where it shouldn't be. Why should Rachel care who he wanted to spend his time with? The guy needed lessons on romantic gestures, and she was positive Andrea's answer would be no.

"Wonderful. We need to set a date. Let's get together for dinner, and we can talk more about it. The sooner, the better, don't you think?" Chad spoke with passion to the woman, and Rachel's seed of jealousy grew.

Andrea said yes. Leslie's matchmaking attempts had just hit a brick wall.

The problem was, it left Rachel far more unsettled than it should have.

She moved further away, trying to zone out the sound of his voice. Pulling out her phone, she wanted to check her emails for the twentieth time that day. The email notification alert announced she had mail. Clicking on the icon, she scanned the sender and the subject line.

The Alaskan Outreach Center. Vacant position opportunity.

She sucked in a deep breath, knowing this was the answer she'd been praying to receive. *Please, Lord, let this be a yes.*

Dear Rachel Harrelson,

We received your application to volunteer with us. There were several qualified candidates for the teaching position, and we've made our decision. We would be delighted to have you on the team. You have excellent references and experience, and we love your passion for God.

Is next week too soon? Once you arrive, all your living and food expenses will be covered, and you'll receive a stipend of one hundred dollars a week for incidentals. I hope this is acceptable and you agree to join the team. Please let us know ASAP.

In Christ Love,
Jonathan Winters

She got the job. A thrill raced through Rachel, chasing out any doubts she was on the right track. God was answering her prayers, and in a way, letting her know all would be okay with Leslie. It felt as though a weight had been lifted from her heart.

"See you tonight, Andrea. We celebrate with a toast," Chad's voice cut into her mental happy dance as he approached.

He was smiling as though a weight had been lifted from his heart as well. Andrea was clearly good for him. "Hey there, I didn't know you were here. Is everything okay with Leslie?"

"Yes. Don't worry. She's taking a nap, and I wanted to let you know before I left to head home." Rachel stood, pocketing her phone.

"Rest is always best for the healing process. Leslie seemed in good spirits, don't you think?" Chad asked.

Seeing his sister in person had clearly done wonders for his attitude. "I agree. Listen, I just wanted to thank you for putting up with me this past week." She thought about shaking his hand, but it seemed too formal. "I'm sure you'll be glad to have me out of your hair and have the cabin to yourself." Rachel leaned forward and hugged him instead, catching Chad off guard.

He hugged her back, and just as quickly, let go. "It'll be quiet, that's for sure," he teased.

"I got an offer from the Alaskan Outreach Center. Best news ever. So everything is working out good for both of us."

Chad was silent for what seemed a long time before he nodded. "Well, I guess this is goodbye then. Congratulations, I'm sure it will be an awesome experience. Send me some wildlife photos, including the ones you took up at the cabin. I'd love to see them. Might even use them in the community center with your permission."

"Thank you. That would be amazing. Alaska was my first pick, so I'm thrilled. I'm leaving next week, and there's so much I need to do to get ready."

Chad leaned down and dropped a kiss on her cheek. "Take care then. I enjoyed getting to know you. Make sure they keep you as far away from the kitchen as possible." He winked.

Rachel was more than a little surprised by the kiss, but she recovered quick enough to laugh, easing the awkwardness. "I'll hang a warning label around my neck." She turned and walked out the door. Away from Chad, and away from the conflicting feeling that she was leaving something important behind.

Chapter Twelve

♥

Knock. Knock.

Rachel headed for the door, but her mother beat her to answer it. They weren't expecting any company that she knew of, and Rachel stood there waiting to see who was dropping by as her mother pulled open the door.

"Hello. I'm Chad McCarthy, and I was wondering if Rachel was here."

Chad? Rachel moved forward.

"Of course you are. You've been gone a while, but I make it my business to know everyone in town," her mother said, a slightly frosty chill to her voice.

"I've got this, Mother," Rachel hastened to rescue Chad.

"I'm sure you do. Just make sure you remember you're engaged, young lady. Act accordingly. It won't do to make Alex jealous, you know." Her mother lifted her chin, turned, and walked off toward the kitchen, but not before she shot an all-knowing look at Rachel to reinforce her directive.

It wasn't even worth correcting her mother. Rachel had no intentions of falling back into a relationship with Alex, but so far, talking to her mother was like talking to a brick wall. "Sorry about that."

Chad frowned. "I didn't realize you were still engaged. Or engaged again. Perhaps I shouldn't have come," he said as he stepped back off the porch.

She shook her head. "I'm not engaged."

Chad stopped and looked up at her, a slightly confused expression on his face.

"And have no plans to get engaged," she continued. "I told you that I'm leaving for Alaska. I've got an early morning flight out of Knoxville next week."

"Then why—"

"It's what I've been telling you." Rachel stepped out on the porch. "My mother has my life planned out one way, and I have a different opinion. It's why I ran away to your cabin on my wedding day. I needed to escape the controlling parents and the sympathetic yet prying eyes of people. It's also why I had to leave again as soon as I could. Otherwise, my mother would have come to chaperone us like two wayward teenagers, making sure we didn't do anything we shouldn't be doing. We wouldn't want to look bad in front of the church's eyes. She gives me no credit for having the ability to make my own decisions." At times, her mother's controlling parental attitude was an embarrassment—like now.

Chad dared to grin. "Not everyone at church is that demanding. People understand life happens. It's more about character than social rules that direct a person to the choices they make."

"Exactly." She nodded. It was nice to have someone understand her side, but Chad talking about church was an exciting change of direction. "I thought you didn't believe in God anymore?"

"It's not that I don't believe. More like that, I don't understand," Chad said quietly.

Rachel stepped forward to touch his arm. "There's no way for us to understand everything, but there is a way for you to trust in God. If he's truly in your heart, he will guide the decisions you make. And although there's no way to know if it's the right road, you can be sure if it's the right road, you'll know it and grow from it. Sometimes, even the wrong roads are about learning something you need to know or understand before the next step of your life."

"I didn't come to talk to you about God. I came to apologize for my rude behavior concerning Leslie. I was already upset thinking you told her about the nightmare you witnessed, seeing as you were more than a little determined to find a way to help me. The fear of losing Leslie hit me hard, and I took my frustration out on you, and I'm sorry." Chad ran a hand through his hair, obviously not comfortable with the conversation.

It took character to own up to your mistakes, and it was sweet of him to show up to make things right before she left. "There's no need to apologize. And for the record, I did tell your sister, but not because I'm a busybody trying to run your life."

Chad shook his head, lines of tension creasing his forehead.

"Before you say anything, please understand; I told her because I care about you. The time we spent together has been special, and I would hate to see you disappear behind a self-imposed wall from all the good you have to offer others. I know you disagree with me, and I'm sorry, but I truly had your best interest at heart."

"My life is my own, and I think I can decide for myself how to deal with it. But thank you for your concern." Diplomatically correct, but off-putting just the same.

Pulling a move from Chad's own playbook, Rachel decided to change the subject. This was one of those agree to disagree matters. "How is Leslie anyway? I was expecting her to call me this morning, but I haven't heard anything yet."

"She did well all night. In fact, I just came from dropping her off at her place. Leslie sent me off with a shopping list, and after that, I plan to stay at her place for the next few days to take care of her."

Rachel's heart soared. "That's great news. Tell her I'll stop by later. On the one hand, I'm thrilled to be headed out on this mission trip, but I hate leaving her again, especially if she needs me. Her car won't even be ready for a week or two, from what I understand." Leslie wouldn't even let her think of putting off leaving for the mission trip, knowing how much she'd wanted this position.

"All taken care of. I got Leslie another vehicle to use if she wants to go anywhere. When she opts to drive again is another story. She was fairly stressed out on the ride home."

Rachel nodded, positive anyone in the same position would find it challenging to jump back in a car and drive. "Understandable."

"Like I said, I wanted to apologize for everything. I've enjoyed getting to know you, even if my attitude and issues can sometimes lead you to believe otherwise." He shifted from one side to the other, his hand tucked in his pockets. "The thing is, Rachel, I care about you more than I expected, and can't help but wonder how things might have gone if you weren't so intent on leaving." His gaze connected with hers and the intensity in his brown eyes wasn't lost on Rachel.

His words set her heart to racing. "I've wondered the same thing, but also know it would have never worked. We're just two friends on different roads," she said, opting for total honesty. If she wasn't leaving, it would be all too easy to follow her heart and let him know she cared more than she was letting on to him or Leslie. *Except Andrea was in the picture big time, something else she needed to remember.*

And giving up on her dream to travel wasn't something Rachel was willing to do, even if Andrea wasn't in the picture. This was her chance at freedom. God had opened the door to independence and happiness, and she was choosing to step through it.

Chad frowned. "Okay, then. I just wanted you to know what was on my mind before you left."

She couldn't let herself get drawn into a web that would rob her of independence and choice, no matter how tempting. And watching Chad with someone else would be far more difficult than she had envisioned. "It's not like you'll be lonely. You've got Andrea to keep you company."

"What does she have to do with anything? There's nothing remotely personal between us. Never mind," Chad said, shaking his head. "You've made your decision to leave, unless, of course, it's more a case of running away. Just like you did with Alex, perhaps?"

Nothing personal wasn't the way Rachel heard his conversation with Andrea, but she was more than willing to give Chad the benefit of the doubt. She just couldn't let it change the direction she'd chosen. And there was no way she would justify Chad's accusation with an answer. She didn't owe him an explanation the last time she checked. "I don't think my personal life is any of your business," she said, trying to keep the hurt out of her voice.

"Fair enough," Chad said as he turned and left.

Chad was wrong. It wasn't the same thing this time around. It was her life, and the mission trips were calling her name.

A door she wanted to open by choice.

Chapter Thirteen

♥

THE WEEK WENT BY all too quickly for Rachel. Leslie was doing great, although still not driving. She'd run into Chad a few times at her friend's house, but he usually made a quick getaway shortly after her arrival. And a couple of days ago he had returned to the solitude of the cabin, with Leslie was back on her feet and doing well. Rachel didn't like the stiff awkwardness that existed between them, but there was nothing she could do about it at this point. Alaska was calling her name.

Rachel called for a shuttle to take her to the airport, not wanting her mother to cancel her Ladies Society meeting. It was a bit pricey for the two-hour trip, but a lot easier way to say goodbye and leave. Her own car had been towed out the ditch, and she'd parked it in one of the garage spaces at her parent's, preferring to keep it in a safe place under cover since she'd be gone another year.

For all her mother's harping on Rachel's life, she also knew her mother loved her and wanted her to be happy. Preferably with someone who was a strong Christian and someone she considered worthy of her daughter.

For Rachel, she simply wanted love. An image of Chad came to mind.

"Can you stop at 2522 Belmont Street on the way out of town?" she asked. "I want to say goodbye to my friend in person."

"Sure thing, Miss," the shuttle driver said. Minutes later, he pulled up in front of Leslie's house.

"I'll just be a minute."

The man grinned. "Take your time; the meter is running."

Rachel hurried up the walkway and knocked on the door.

It wasn't long before Leslie answered. "I wasn't expecting to see you this morning," Leslie said, glancing at the waiting taxi and then stepping back to let Rachel inside.

"Couldn't leave without seeing my bestie." Rachel pulled Leslie in for a hug, being careful of her casted arm.

"I'm going to miss you. Are you sure you have to go now? I mean, I know you've wanted Alaska ever since you started doing mission work, but you just got home."

Rachel nodded. "Yes. God opened the door for me to go to my dream location. Clearly, I'm needed, maybe as much for the children there, as for my own personal growth." At least, that's what she kept telling herself every time a deep feeling settled in the pit of her stomach...one that made her feel she was missing something important.

"What about Chad? You two seem to have connected, and when he's here, he's always asking about you. I know my brother, and he's interested, even if he hasn't admitted it. Maybe there's something here for you also—another door."

The problem was—he had hinted at possible feelings. Rachel had mulled over the admission but wasn't willing to let the idea gain traction. There was too much uncertainty and thoughts like that could derail a person, and she was finally on track. "Wishful thinking. I think Chad is interested in someone named Andrea." Chad had said otherwise, and Rachel mostly believed him. Seeing as it didn't matter, Rachel hadn't pressed the issue.

"What are you talking about? When? I'm sure he would have told me," Leslie insisted.

Rachel hadn't asked for a clarification of his comment simply because she was afraid of his answer. If he wasn't spoken for, there were all sorts of room for Rachel to get crazy ideas in her head. Ideas that could stop her from leaving, letting her heart run away with actions. "Maybe I was wrong. Either way, I've got to go. Wouldn't want to miss my flight. Love you," Rachel said, heading down the steps before Leslie had a chance to convince her to do something drastic—like stay.

"Love you too. Call me when you land," Leslie called right back.

"Will do." Rachel climbed into the taxi, brushing away the tears running down her face. "Let's go."

The driver wound his way through the streets and made his way to the airport. Leslie's words confirmed what Rachel suspected Chad had meant when he said there was nothing personal between him and Andrea. He wasn't engaged, or even in a relationship, for that matter. It was the confirmation she'd been avoiding for reasons of her own.

She picked up her phone...wanting to call Chad.

No. Rachel slid the phone back into her purse and closed her eyes. It was better this way. The mission trip was her dream, and no matter what Chad thought, Rachel wasn't running away. *Was she?*

Leaving on the mission trip after her engagement to Alex *had* been running—she knew that now. And it was entirely possible her newest trip was giving her an excuse not to enter a relationship. But Rachel refused to let any man change her life and the course she had set for herself, at least not now that she was free of Alex.

The last thing she wanted to do was to give a man control over her life. She didn't want to be like her parents. The perfect society wife. The perfect church member. Perfect everything...

She paid the driver and hurried through security. Stopping at Leslie's had cut her arrival a little too close, and they had already begun the boarding process. Rachel handed her ticket to the agent at the gate.

The woman smiled, scanning the boarding pass. "Welcome aboard, miss," she said when it beeped to acknowledge she was cleared to board.

"Thank you." Rachel wheeled her carry-on bag down the gateway. She paused, turning back, the tiny seed of doubt growing. Then, letting out a deep breath, she moved forward and stepped into the plane, keeping the line of passengers moving.

After finding her seat, she waited for everyone else to get situated. The first leg of her journey was about to begin. She pulled out her phone to text Leslie and her mother, letting them know she'd made it on time and was about to take off, and to send them her love.

Rachel accidentally hit the photo button and her screen populated with the most recent gallery of pictures taken. Pictures of Chad. The cabin. Hiking in the woods. Sledding. Other memories surfaced. An image of the two of them laughing and playing backgammon flashed before her. And when he fired his gun into the air to save her from the bear. And the two of them cooking together—and burning breakfast.

She shoved the images aside, intent on saying a prayer for a safe flight, something she did before every takeoff. This time she added a prayer for Chad, hoping he would seek help to make peace with his past. Next, she added one for Leslie for continued healing, and then one for Alex. Looking back, she was happy he had been brave enough to put an end to the madness, and only wished him happiness.

Finished, a warm glow filled her, and she settled back in her seat.

Tell him how you feel. The words came out of nowhere, but Rachel knew the source. A message from God wasn't one you ignored. Not one to ignore such a direct message, she vowed to call Chad when she landed. The man had been through so much in the military, and his reactions were those of someone on edge. Someone afraid to lose his sister. She'd forgiven him, but had he forgiven himself? His responses still said no, and Rachel wanted better for him—because she cared.

Truth be told, she'd fallen in love with him. An emotion she hadn't put a name to—until now.

Tears filled her eyes, and Rachel brushed them away.

Caring was one thing. Love asked for more between two people. A willingness to put his needs above her own while at the same time still being true to oneself. The question was, how did one make it all happen? And if it was real, wouldn't it all wait until she returned a year from now?

More tears soon replaced the others. Rachel reached for a tissue, unable to stop the emotions rushing through her.

Are you running again?

Chad had been right. She was running from the truth. Rachel wanted to put Chad first, proof her feelings were more profound and deeply etched on her heart. She needed to discover if Chad felt the same way or if she was on a fool's errand. Right now, she felt like a runaway fool. But God had opened more than one door for her, and the trouble was choosing which one was right. Rachel sniffed, a fresh barrage of tears falling unchecked.

"Ladies and gentlemen, we apologize for the short delay in leaving but we are waiting on one passenger. No connecting flights will be affected as we can make this time up in the air. Thank you for your patience," the flight attendant's voice was crisp and efficient as she delivered the news.

Rachel's heart pounded in her chest.

Love above all. It was a risky choice, but perhaps one worth a shot. She could always catch another flight to Alaska, but she might never get another chance to tell Chad how she really felt.

Was it possible God was giving her the opportunity to change her decision to leave with the delay? There was only one way to find out. Rachel unfastened her seat belt. "Excuse me, I need to get off the plane."

The flight attendant shook her head. "You need to sit down, miss. We're about to take off and only just waiting for one late passenger. We won't have time to let you back on as we are ready to close the door and taxi down the runway."

"That's fine. I'll catch another flight." Rachel brushed away her tears, grabbed her carry-on bag from the overhead bin, and raced off the plane. With each step back up the gateway, her heart felt lighter. There was unfinished business here, and she wasn't running away. Not anymore. Staying an extra day may change nothing at all, but it was something she had to discover for herself.

Rushing into the waiting area, she glanced around, looking for the exit sign. Rachel took a step forward, only to run into a passenger making a beeline for the gateway.

"I'm sorry," she said, stopping to regroup and look up at the man, shocked to discover Chad standing there.

"Rachel?" He asked, his expression more than a little comical and most likely a mirror of her own. "I thought you left. I thought I was too late," he said, his voice low and filled with emotion.

Chad was here—at the airport. *For her.*

Too late? Never. Rachel threw her arms around his neck and kissed him, not wanting to miss another opportunity to show him how she felt.

"Now that's the kind of hello a man could get used to." Chad grinned.

The gate agent came to stand next to them. "Excuse me, sir. You need to get on the plane. They can't hold the flight any longer, and I've got to close the door."

Rachel frowned. "On the plane? Where are you going?"

"I was headed to Alaska. With you," Chad said, his eyes glowing with an emotion she was almost afraid to identify.

"You were? Why?" she asked, wanting desperately to hear the words.

"Because wherever you are is where I want to be. Have you been crying?" Chad asked, his tone concerned as he touched her face, letting his thumb wipe away a tear.

"Yes. I know it's silly," Rachel said, holding up her tissue. "I just couldn't stop them. I'm an emotional wreck. Over you."

"Now I know you care. You didn't cry the day I met you and that was a rough day for you as I recall. And judging by your kiss, I'm guessing you're okay with me tagging along to Alaska."

They both knew the day he was referring to, and he was right—she hadn't cried. More proof she was doing the right thing this time around and that she genuinely cared about Chad. "But what about the community center?" Rachel asked. The program was needed and would be such a huge blessing to others, and it was one she didn't want to stand in the way of.

Chad smiled, his eyes crinkling at the corners. "Being with you is where I need to be. I can manage the community center remotely for the time being. It'll just take a little longer."

"Or we could both stay here and I could help you. You did ask me once to manage the place. Is the job offer still open?"

He shook his head, his grin widening. "No. But I think the position of girlfriend is available. Any interest in sticking around to find out?"

Rachel wrapped her arms around his neck, her heart overflowing with love. "Absolutely. There will be other mission trips but being with you is the most important part of my life."

"Are you sure? Alaska is your dream."

"Yes, I'm sure. The Outreach Center has fifty applications for every position. They will have no problem filling the position, whereas you're needed here. This is important too and something we can share together."

"Sir?" the agent asked, her voice one of urgency.

"Sorry. You can close the door. I'm happy right where I am." Chad lowered his head to kiss Rachel, sealing the deal.

"I still can't believe you're here." Rachel shook her head, her heart overflowing with joy.

"I still can't believe you just missed your flight. For me." Chad pulled her close, lifting her off the ground to twirl her around.

"For us," she said, as he set her down. "I kept thinking of all the fun we shared, and how much we had in common, and how perhaps God brought us together for this very reason."

"And here I was thinking it was simply my charm," Chad teased. "I was at the community center and realized my reasons to settle in one place weren't good enough and they wouldn't bring me the happiness and joy I shared while spending time with you. I didn't want to lose you by running scared from life and love. I want to give us a chance to discover where a relationship might lead us."

"Sounds to me like we both came to our senses."

Chad swung her carry-on bag over his shoulder, adding it to his own. He took her free hand and together they made their way through the airport—like two people in love.

When Chad stopped to use the restroom, Rachel called the Alaskan Outreach Center to let them know her change in plans. She had a moment's trepidation, but it didn't last long once the coordinator assured Rachel she'd been right—there were plenty of applicants all too willing to fill the vacancy.

As she and Chad left the airport, Rachel know they'd have to work out the details of getting the rest of their luggage back, but for now, she wanted to bask in the revelation that trusting in God had brought them together.

Chapter Fourteen

♥

RACHEL SQUINTED AS THEY exited the terminal into the bright sunlight, drawing her jacket tighter against the cold.

"We need to take a taxi back into town," Chad said, smiling down at her.

"Why didn't you drive?" she asked.

"I wasn't sure how long I'd be gone. Being with you was all that mattered." Chad grinned as he signaled for a taxi.

The open honesty and warmth in his comment filled her with a sense of peace. "That's a lovely thing to say, especially because I believe you mean it."

"Actions speak louder than words and I intend to keep showing you how much you mean to me."

"Sounds good." She laughed.

The taxi pulled up to the curb and they slid in the back seat. Chad gave the address of the community center to the driver.

"So what's happening with the program? I would have thought at this stage of the planning it would be impossible for you to go anywhere," Rachel asked.

"The program is in good hands, trust me. My new manager has loads of experience, and she is well suited to handling everything once the place is up and running and all the proper staff is hired."

"She?" Rachel asked, zeroing in on the one word and unable to stop the question, even if it did sound a tad jealous.

"Andrea." Chad winked.

Yikes. "Oh, Andrea." It was a perfectly good explanation for everything she'd overheard, and it explained Chad's *not personal* comment. It was only Rachel who hadn't wanted to know the truth out of fear it would affect her decision to leave town—something that happened anyway. "You could have told me."

"I tried. I told you there was nothing personal between us. Just business. What else would there be?

Although, I do like that you were a little jealous." Chad chuckled, as he kissed the back of her hand tenderly.

"Okay, wise guy. But from now on, full disclosure, right?" If they were going to be a team, it would require working together from every aspect. Talking and actions went hand in hand with trust. And love.

"Absolutely." They arrived at the center, and Chad helped her out of the car. They headed inside, where a beautiful brunette met them halfway across the huge gym where workers were busy laying a new floor.

"Andrea, I'd like you to meet Rachel. My girlfriend." Chad hadn't let go of her hand.

"It's nice to finally meet you. I've heard so much about you, and I'm so happy Chad stepped up and announced his feelings for you. If you two hadn't settled your differences soon, I was going to pay Rachel a visit in Alaska myself to see if I could talk some sense into one of you." Andrea exuded a confidence and an energy that fully explained why Chad wanted her as his manager.

Chad frowned. "I wasn't that bad."

"You were a bear," Andrea quipped, shaking her head.

"I get that." Rachel grinned. "Totally. The bears do seem to be active this time of year, more than some would think," she teased. Her encounter with a real bear wasn't something she wanted to repeat, but Chad, she could deal with him every now and then, as long as they were together.

Andrea would do wonders with the organization. Rachel wasn't manager material, but she would love to run one of the activities at some point. One that would grow and serve multitudes of children, helping them to find their way to God and through life in general.

"Why don't you show Rachel around and point out the changes we are going to make?" Andrea suggested. "I need to meet with the builder to make some small modifications to the plans and make sure we are on schedule. The grand opening needs to happen on time because I've already got twenty-two kids signed up to attend the basketball camp."

"I knew hiring you was a good idea. Leaves me free to pay more attention to something equally important and far more demanding." Chad laughed, pulling Rachel close.

"Am not! Demanding, that is," Rachel challenged. *Important*, that was something she'd take all day long.

Chad grinned, not letting her move away. "Oh yeah, then what was—*sleep on the couch, clean the dishes, split the wood, get counseling*, and a number of any other things you wanted me to do?"

She was surprised when he mentioned counseling in front of Andrea, and it caught her off guard. "Counseling?" she asked, zeroing in on the single most valuable part of his teasing.

Andrea walked away, her hands waving at the men who had taken over the focus of her attention.

"Yes. I thought about what you said and scheduled my first appointment. After talking with the doctor, I agreed with you. I even told Andrea about the PTSD, figuring that since we would be working closely together, it was something she ought to know. Seems you were right about a lot of things," he admitted, leaning in to kiss her on the cheek.

Thank you, Lord. Rachel couldn't have guessed the path life would take, but she'd trusted in God, and it was working out better than expected. "Just keep remembering that. Especially when I march you to church with me next Sunday."

"Let's not get carried away," Chad said.

Rachel brushed her hair back off her face and shot him one of those we-will-see looks. "I understand the art of compromise, and we are a team now. Right? So if not this Sunday, then next Sunday."

Chad shook his head, but his smile said just the opposite. "You aren't going to let me win this one either, are you?"

"That's where you're wrong. If you come to church with me, it's you who wins." Growing up, she hadn't always felt the same connection with the church the way she did now. As an adult, she understood not every church was perfect. Nor would it ever be since it included people. Imperfect people trying to do better in a world that struggled for love and happiness.

"How's that?" he asked.

"You will meet some really great people who live in the community. People who will support you and support your project. And best of all, people who will help you discover your own personal relationship with God. There are small groups, and I'm sure there will be one you will like and fit into if you give it a chance. It's all about taking the first step with a leap of faith. Surrounding yourself with other people who want love and happiness, and a support team when we stumble." Rachel was passionate about her approach to Christianity. And although she found herself wavering at times, it was the support team at her church who helped get her through the rough patches and to keep her eye on what was most important.

God.

"I'm already getting that with you. You did get me into counseling, after all," Chad teased.

"Okay, then...the second step." She laughed. The only thing she regretted was missing out on the Alaskan mission trip. Still, if it was truly in God's plan for her life, there would be another opportunity.

They walked around the building, and Chad pointed out areas and explained the changes he wanted to implement, his vision clear and poignant. The passion with which he spoke when he talked about the kids was one of the things that drew her to him in the first place. Now, more than ever, she felt connected in a way she hadn't thought possible.

They exited through the back door. "There's my truck," Chad said, pointing to a black SUV parked there. "Where to next? I feel like we need to do something fun. Something crazy to mark today as extra special."

"It's already extra special, seeing as I just deboarded a plane to find you, only to discover you were coming to find me. So I'd say that's memory-worthy." It would undoubtedly be a day she would never forget.

"It is," he agreed, kissing her lightly on the mouth.

"I'd like to drop by Leslie's. Telling her about the change in planes in person and seeing the look on her face, is simply too hard to resist. After that, I'm all yours."

"I like the sound of that." He opened the passenger door and helped her inside. Pausing, he took her hand in his. "Rachel, I truly hope this won't leave the Outreach in a bind. I mean, if we need to go, we go. Helping others is more important, no matter what form it takes. I need you to know this. I don't want to take away your dream."

It was more proof Chad was the right man for her—the one God intended. "I agree, but in this instance, I've done someone else a huge favor."

"What do you mean?" he asked.

"Alaska is a very competitive market when it comes to getting a volunteer position. I called them while you were in the men's room at the airport to let them know my plans changed and apologized. They had quite a few candidates and were totally fine with my decision. I'd like to think I made someone else's dream come true, as well as my own. God works in mysterious ways."

"That he does." Chad smiled. "I think I'm beginning to understand that, thanks to you. You are the most upbeat, positive person I know."

Rachel beamed. It was one of the nicest compliments she'd ever received. "And you're the most amazing, giving, determined man I know."

"Guess that's why we make a good team." Chad slid in the driver's seat, started the truck, and they headed toward Leslie's.

He suddenly braked and pulled into a parking spot. "I've got an idea, one I think you'll like," his boyish enthusiasm was more than enough to sell her on the idea without even knowing what he wanted to do."

"Sounds good to me," she said simply, putting her trust in whatever it was Chad was cooking up.

"Perfect. I'll be right back," he said, sliding out of the truck. Moments later, he entered the deli.

Good. Whatever it was he was planning didn't involve him doing any of the cooking.

Rachel decided to call her mother, but it rolled to voicemail. Talk about good luck. "Hey, Mom. Just wanted to let you know there's been a change in plans, and I'm not headed to Alaska. At least not yet. I'll explain lat—"

"Rachel? Are you still there?" her mother asked in a breathless voice like she'd run for the phone.

Apparently, Rachel's luck was short-lived. "Yes. I just left you a message letting you know I'm not leaving for Alaska." She waited for the slew of questions, followed by the lecture that would come.

"Oh dear, why not?" her mother asked, her tone concerned.

Not at all the response or tone she expected from her mother. "Change of plans." Now wasn't the time to explain about Chad or her reasons for taking a detour in life to take a chance on love. Something she wasn't willing to do for Alex. At least now, she understood why she left. It was merely a wait to buy time against the inevitably lousy decision when she said yes to Alex in the first place.

"Oh, dear," her mother's echoed words left Rachel in a quandary of how to continue.

"What's wrong, Mom? You keep saying, *oh, dear*. Like you wanted me to go, something we both know isn't true. I thought you'd be happy I was sticking around." She glanced up at the deli, relieved to see Chad wasn't in sight. Her mother was acting strange, and she didn't want anything to dampen her afternoon with Chad.

"I am, dear. You see, though. I mean, the thing is...well, I just came from the grocery store. I ran into Alex there, and I, oh dear, I know you don't want me talking about it, but—"

"Mom, there's nothing between Alex and me." This one-track line of thinking on her mother's part had to stop.

"That's good, dear. So good. Because Alex was with that wedding planner of yours–that Brittany girl. Can you believe it? They were holding hands, and…and then he kissed her. I'm so sorry, dear."

Her mother's concern was genuine, and it went a long way to lifting the cloud hanging over them. She was finally accepting the truth—or what she knew of it anyway. It was up to Rachel to fill in the blanks seeing as the breakup wasn't entirely Alex's fault.

"I know all about it, Mom. I told you, Alex and I talked. We weren't meant to be together. We never were. It was just two people following expectations and not their hearts. Alex is in love with Brittany, and I'm happy for him. For them. Everything had worked out for the best, trust me." Especially the part where Rachel herself was giving love a real shot—not running away.

"You knew?" her mother asked.

"Yes. After I left the wedding, I called Alex on the way to the cabin, and we talked. Alex asked me not to say anything until he had time to break the news to his parents. I'm guessing by now, they know. But then, it sounds like everyone knows, which is good."

"I so wanted you to find love. Marriage is a blessing, and children are another of God's beautiful blessings if they're anything like you. So I just want you to be happy," her mother said, emotion choking her voice.

This was a side of her mother she rarely saw, but it was always welcome. "I am happy, Mother. And just so you know, I've met someone. And as far as new beginnings go in a relationship, I'd say this one has strong prospects." Of course, she wouldn't go as far as Leslie vocally with regards to marriage, but deep down, Rachel couldn't help the secret hope her friend was right.

"Oh. Who is he, dear?"

"Chad McCarthy." Speaking of the handsome new man in her life, he was walking out of the deli, a large basket in hand. A picnic would be perfect—especially with him.

"Leslie's brother is a fine young man. Just home from Afghanistan and doing some wonderful things at the community center. It's all over town. We should have him over to dinner." And just like that, her mother had moved on.

Only the new cycle wouldn't end until Rachel was walking down the aisle, but in the case of Chad, she didn't mind. "That sounds lovely, Mother."

"Wait until I tell your father. He'll be thrilled his little girl has found someone of her own."

Rachel wasn't so little anymore, but she'd always be her daddy's little girl. Something totally okay with her. "I've got to run. Chad is back from an errand, and he has a surprise planned."

"Oh, how sweet. A man who likes surprises is a real gem."

Her matchmaking mother was on a roll, something only time would tell if her new boyfriend was up to.

Chad returned, sliding the basket in the back seat.

"What's with the basket?" she asked.

"I thought we should have a romantic picnic at the cabin. Kind of like a first date." He grinned.

A die-hard romantic was not something she'd pegged him for, but it was totally appealing. "But we've eaten there plenty of times."

Chad shook his head. "Not any food this good, and, I might add, not voluntarily. This is all by choice since we are officially in a relationship."

"I thought food was the way to a man's stomach, not the other way around?" Rachel laughed, basking in the glow of his sweet intentions.

"I think it definitely works both ways when neither of us knows how to cook," he teased.

He was right of course. Not to mention, it sounded like the perfect way to commemorate the changes and decisions made today that would affect the course of their future.

Chapter Fifteen

♥

C HAD PULLED UP TO Leslie's house and parked next to the curb. They slid out of the car and cut across the lawn, heading for the porch.

Knock. Knock.

Rachel shot Chad a grin, more than a little excited to share the news with her friend.

The front door was pulled open, and Leslie stood there gawking at her. "You do realize you're supposed to be on a plane? What happened? You said you were on board waiting to take off." she said, getting right to the point.

There was no need for pleasant formalities between friends, and this was big news. The biggest. "Actually, I did. Miss it, that is. On purpose." She took great pleasure in unfolding the news layer by layer.

"What? I can't believe that. That's not like you at all, Miss Efficient. What happened? And more importantly, when can you get another flight to Alaska? And how is it Chad's with you?" she asked, darting a glance at her brother who'd stood off to the side, equally wanting to enjoy his sisters reaction when she learned the truth. Brother and sister, always looking to one-up each other. And this new development certainly fit the category.

Leslie had a lot to worry about, but Rachel wasn't one of the worries, or shouldn't be. It wouldn't do to keep Leslie in suspense. "Slow down and let me tell you what happened."

"Then hurry up, will you. You sound far too happy and easy-going about all this."

Rachel laughed. "The thing is, I was on the plane. But as I was sitting there waiting for the doors to close, I said my prayers. You know, the way I always do. And when I finished, everything changed. There was a short delay in our departure, and suddenly, I knew I had to get off the plane." There was so much more to it, but it was hard to explain the urgency and strong feeling guiding her decision. How did one explain taking a risk for a feeling?

"Oh, no. What did you do, Rachel Harrelson? Did you cause a ruckus and get arrested? Is that why Chad's here? Did he bail you out of jail?"

"No, nothing like that." Her friend had a vivid imagination. "I got off the plane voluntarily," she said, putting Leslie at ease. It wouldn't do to have her racing out the door to face down airport security, all for the sake of prolonging the good news.

"Why?" Leslie demanded.

Rachel smiled. "You have my permission to say I told you so because the answer to your question is simple. Chad."

He stepped forward and reached for Rachel's hand, a happy grin on his face.

Rachel waited for the information to sink in.

"As in Chad and you? *Ummm*, together?" she asked, glancing down at their interlocked hands. Leslie's eyes grew wide, twinkling like lights on a Christmas tree.

"Yes. Together," Chad said, pulling Rachel close.

"You were right about how I felt toward him, and I decided I wasn't going to run away without letting Chad know the truth," Rachel explained. "But listen to this...the kicker is...it turns out your brother was getting on the plane. To Alaska."

"So if you're both going to Alaska, why are you still here? I'm having a hard time keeping up with you two, but I like what I'm seeing." She grinned.

"We were going. I planned on traveling to Alaska with Rachel and working remotely at the community center. Staying here, for the time being, will help get the program on its feet faster," Chad said, trying to bring Leslie up to speed.

Rachel was still giddy when she thought of the moment she ran into him outside the gateway. It was a memory she would cherish forever. "I plan on helping at the community center while he gets it up and running with Andrea—his new manager," Rachel said emphasizing the last word, knowing that once upon a time she'd thought the woman's role in Chad's life was something completely different. She wanted her friend to know the truth of the matter.

"Woohoo! I knew I was right. Told you so, girlfriend." Leslie pulled her in for a hug, raising her casted arm in the air and out of the way.

This was the easy-going, laughing Leslie that she knew and loved. Maybe the news was the best medicine to helping her friend recover from the accident. Rachel grinned, more than willing to give Leslie credit for calling the relationship between her and Chad right. "Yes, you did."

Leslie squealed. "We're going to be real sisters. And I get to be the maid of honor. And we get to plan a wedding. Oh, such fun. Yay!"

"Not so fast. There aren't any wedding bells, just an agreement to date. You need to slow down your expectations by at least a year or two," Rachel joked, trying to rein her friend's enthusiasm down a notch. She snuck a glance at Chad, hoping Leslie's wedding bell enthusiasm wouldn't send him running for the hills.

"A month or two tops," Leslie insisted.

"That's enough, Leslie. Quit pushing us. Rachel's had enough of that to last a lifetime. We'll take this as fast or as slow as we need to, but it will be right for the both of us. And right now, I've got plans to take my girlfriend on a romantic picnic if you'll quit jabbering away about a wedding." Chad chuckled. He leaned in and gave his sister a hug. "I'll be in the truck waiting, Rachel, so don't let her talk your ear off."

"So that's how you want to play it. *Hmmpphh.* We'll see. As to a picnic, as long as Chad's not doing the cooking, you're safe," Leslie teased, as they both watched him walk away.

"That's exactly what I thought earlier. I learned that the hard way—from experience. But then again, who am I to talk? Neither one of us can cook." Maybe there is a lot of dining out in the near future. The memory of the burned breakfast fiasco not one she or Chad would forget anytime soon.

"*Ohhh*, that gives me a great wedding gift idea. A cookbook and cooking lessons for two. It would be perfect," Leslie announced.

Leave it to her friend to jump to the finish line even after she'd been warned to stop. "Leslie, knock it off. No wedding plans are in the making. You've got to stop this nonsense. You know the old saying...walk before you run. That's what we've agreed to do."

"Sure thing, sis. I need to go research cooking lessons, and you need to go on a picnic. Later," Leslie said, stepping back into the house and closing the door. Her friend was on a one-way track down the wedding aisle—for her brother and best friend, and it would seem there was no derailing the train.

"Everything okay?" he asked tenderly when she climbed into the truck.

"Let's see, your sister has got us married in two-or-three months tops. Oh, and my mother, well she has you coming to Sunday dinner. And in case you didn't know it, you're the new paragon in town and her top pick for my boyfriend, soon-to-be husband."

Chad laughed. "All sounds good to me," he said, starting the truck and putting it into gear, treating her comment as if she were talking about nothing more than the weather.

"Quit teasing," she said, punching him in the arm. She'd told him the truth more as a way to take the pressure off when the reality of the matchmaking efforts of his sister and her mom hit him hard. But it would seem it backfired...his answer sending her heart racing and her brain into overdrive. "So tell me what you have in mind for our date? We've got lots of time to kill on the drive up to the cabin."

"I hadn't gotten that far in the planning." He grinned. "It was impromptu."

"Well, okay then. We can plan it out to make the best use of our time and make sure we leave in time to get home. How about a walk in the woods? Or we could even try sledding again. That was so much fun. But then, it has recently occurred to me that everything I do with you seems better somehow." It was also the reason she'd started to wonder if things were different between them than any other relationship she'd been in because, in the past, it never worked out this way.

"Not worried about running into another bear?" Chad teased.

"Not with you around. My hero would save me every time." He'd been doing it ever since they met, he just didn't know it, and she hadn't even realized it herself until recently.

"That I would," he said, reaching over to cover her hand with his, their fingers intertwining.

They arrived at the cabin, the place freezing cold since Chad had closed the place intending to head to Alaska. His actions still had the power to leave her in awe. What woman wouldn't be flattered? "*Brrr,*" she said, pulling her coat tight around her and jumping up and down to get her circulation going for warmth.

"Sorry, I should have remembered this part. I'll have a fire started in no time," Chad said, moving to the fireplace. He bent down to light the starter log he'd placed in between the larger pieces of wood.

"Good idea. I would have thought a rough and tumble former-military man would have started his own fire. You know…like a boy scout," she teased.

"Except boy scouts grow into men and become a master scout leader. Any good leader recognizes the benefit of making a job easier and quicker, especially for someone he…cares about deeply." A warm light reflected in his eyes as he gazed down at her.

The pause in his comment set Rachel's heart in racing mode as she wondered what he'd been about to say, but for now, she'd let it slide. *Cared deeply* were strong words and a sentiment she, herself, echoed about him. "Touché. I'll buy that."

Within minutes, the logs had flames licking up, and soon they would put off heat. "I'll grab a couple of blankets, and we can sit by the fire for lunch. Hopefully, the heat pump is in auxiliary mode and gets us up to speed quicker." Cooler temperatures were by design in restaurants that wanted you to eat and run, making way for more guests. Rachel didn't want to speed up anything about this picnic scenario.

"Pricey wish, but for you, it's all worth it," he grinned, moving to the thermostat, and turning the dial higher.

They talked and laughed, the fireside picnic romantic and heartwarming.

Heartwarming enough that Rachel didn't mind the cold. As long as she was together with Chad, her life would always be rich and warm, at least she hoped it would. She didn't want to get ahead of herself, considering this was only their first date. But it was hard not to when one considered the history of their non-date time. A time of friendship with difficulties, and a time that led them to this point. *The care-deeply point.*

"Ready for that walk in the woods?" he asked, rising to his feet as he offered her his hand to help her up.

"I am. Maybe I'll get some great photos. There's always so much to see out here."

"And I'll let you lead so that maybe I get some great snapshots of you. I'm hoping the snow dumps on your head, so I get a turn to laugh." He chuckled, dropping a light kiss on her cheek. "Might even have to make it happen."

Rachel shook her head. "You wouldn't dare. Would you?"

"Guess you'll have to wait and see just what I would or wouldn't do. It's half the fun," Chad said, his warm smile leaving her without a doubt just precisely what he would do.

"Chad..."

"Come on," he said, pulling her forward to where they laid their jackets and stored their boots.

It's not like she wouldn't go, so she'd find out soon enough. It wasn't long before they came to the edge of the woods, and Rachel stopped to take a picture of a fox they spotted through the bare trees. They both stayed quiet, appreciating the moment, and snapping photos to capture the memory.

Snow fell from the branches above her head. "Oh, you brat." She spun to look at Chad through the snow clinging to her eyelids and brushed at her face.

"What? Call it fate, if you will, but I had nothing to do with it. I promise." He chuckled.

"Yeah, right." Rachel leaned down to pick up a handful of snow. *Payback time.*

"Don't you do it." Another pile of snow fell from a branch and landed on his head, his expression becoming one of shock. "No way." Chad brushed the snow off the top of his head and face.

"Fate. I believe you now." She dropped the snow she held in her hand to prove her point.

"Good. Glad we're on the same team," Chad said, taking a step closer.

Rachel nodded. "I agree."

Chad leaned in and kissed her lightly.

But there was nothing light about the sense of well-being and joy she felt. Peaceful. "I think we should move out from under the trees if we don't want another dousing. With the weather warming up, we could get pummeled by the falling snow."

"I don't know. It seems as though it's half the fun." Chad pulled her into his arms, brushing more snow off her hat and out of her hair.

"The other half is being with you," she said, knowing it was true.

"I'd like to think life will be an adventure with the two of us together. What do you think?"

"I couldn't agree more. But does that mean you're still open to making a mission trip with me?" Rachel asked, hoping he'd say yes. In her heart, she still wanted to travel and do mission work. She just wanted to do it side-by-side with Chad.

He nodded. "I wouldn't want it any other way. Compromising is easy if we're together."

Rachel felt relieved. It would seem life was opening doors that all seem to lead to the same place this time around. "Well, then, Mr. McCarthy, you have yourself a date."

"I'm already on a date."

"Yes...but I'm referring to a date with a future. God brought us together, and if we trust him, everything will be okay. Not perfect, but okay."

"*Love, peace, and joy, and the greatest of these is love.* I tend to agree," Chad said, suddenly quoting scripture.

"Wow. Where did that come from? I mean, I love it. And for the record, I agree with the apostle Paul on that one." Love, peace, and joy did all go hand in hand. And love would see one through the hard times.

"Someone once told me to trust in God." He took her by the hand, recalling her words. "And to know God, I had to start reading the Bible. I'm learning so many things and beginning to understand so many truths. Truths I conveniently shoved aside when they didn't suit me," Chad said, his voice ringing sincerity.

"When the truths don't suit you, is when you need God the most to guide you."

"I understand that now. Thank you for caring enough to point me in the right direction."

Rachel wanted to leap for joy. All the things she wanted from life were coming true. The love of God, and the love of a man who cared deeply enough to face his own fears and shortcomings. Peace from sharing a future with someone who loved God as much as she did. Joy knowing she would still travel and have a family and all the many blessings they could share together and in helping others.

God had pushed her in Chad's direction for a reason, and now, Rachel knew without any doubt that reason was love. It was time to be bold and stand up for what she believed in, and she believed in Chad. In them. "I love you," she said, revealing the truth in her heart.

He pulled her in for a hug, gazing down at her. "Good, because I love you, too." Chad kissed her, a beautiful kiss filled with emotion and tenderness.

"You do?" Rachel asked, just as another blob of snow landed on top of them. They pulled apart, laughing and sputtering, brushing the snow off their faces.

Chad reached into his pocket and pulled out his phone. He leaned in next to her and snapped a selfie of them together. "This way, we always have a together memory of laughter."

"Oh, I'm sure we'll have lots of those."

"Good. It's always been said laughter is the best medicine, and I'm betting on it. And to answer your question, of course, I do. Love you, that is. Why else would I be willing to walk away from the community center and follow you to Alaska?"

"Because you have Andrea," she teased. Which didn't matter to Rachel. Either way, he'd made a choice to join her.

Chad shook his head. "There is that, but it's mainly because wherever you are, is where I belong."

Hand in hand, they walked back to the cabin and into their future.

Epilogue

THREE MONTHS LATER...

Life around the community center had been more than enough to keep everyone busy. It had been full speed ahead, and like clockwork, Andrea, Chad, and Rachel worked together to pull off the grand opening in style.

Leave it to Chad, though, to have his own agenda with a surprise. One Rachel knew nothing about until it happened. The perfect wedding proposal. One with stars twinkling from the ceiling, a full moon dangling above the candlelit table set for two, soft piano-jazz music that whispered of love, and all set up in the middle of the community center gymnasium. A place where hundreds of people could have been during the first game, but instead, Chad had proven to give his declaration of love with just the two of them present. It showed how well he understood and loved her, knowing the issues she'd faced when Alex had proposed. There was nothing rushed about Chad's proposal, and most importantly, there was no pressure to say yes.

The night before the grand opening, he'd summoned her to the gym on the pretext of a problem with one of the alarms, and when she arrived the truth was quickly set into motion. It had been a private moment between two people in love, as he went down on one knee and proposed. Rachel had said yes, as there was no other answer in her heart, and Chad had slid the most beautiful diamond on her ring finger, professing his love and then rising to his feet to kiss her. Taking her in his arms, they slow danced, celebrating the magical moment—one she would cherish forever.

The following morning at the grand opening ceremony, Chad had made the announcement to everyone who had come for the ribbon cutting. Kissing her in front of the crowd, the cheers and clapping were thunderous as the town signaled their approval. Her mother, of course, right in the front of the crowd, handkerchief in hand as tears of happiness flowed.

And now, today was another happy day. The happiest of happy days.

Her wedding day.

It turned out Leslie was wrong when she proclaimed they'd be married within two months, but she was close. One month of dating. Two months of engagement. And a lifetime of love. Sounded like a romance made in heaven.

Her father joined her in the vestibule. "Ready, sweetheart?"

"Ready." Rachel grinned, taking one last look at the beautiful wedding dress her mother had help her pick out and pay for. An apology gift for shoving her daughter toward a loveless marriage was how she phrased it. Chad, it would seem, had made quite an impression on her parents.

The organ music started, filling the church with the Bridal Chorus, the sound resonating through the room and filling her heart with joy and hope for the future. Their future.

Leslie hugged Rachel, then turned, and started down the aisle.

This was it. Rachel and her father followed, Rachel smiling at the well-wishers who had come to share in their happiness and celebrate their marriage. Then, gazing down the aisle at her soon-to-be-husband, the love shining in his eyes was like a beacon as she walked toward him. She brushed away her tears of joy, not wanting to miss a single second.

Her father laid her hand on Chad's arm and kissed her cheek. "She's all yours. Take good care of my baby," he said, his eyes glistening with tears.

"Yes, sir. Absolutely," Chad said, earning a clap on the back right before her father took a seat with her mother.

Her mother, of course, already had total need of a handkerchief, and Rachel wasn't far behind.

"Hey, you," she whispered, needing the connection.

"You look stunning," Chad whispered in her ear, giving her hand a squeeze.

They turned to face the pastor. The ceremony was a blessing by God on their future together as they said their vows, pledging to love and cherish each other forever. If there was a way to slow down time, Rachel would do it—this moment genuinely perfect.

"I now pronounce you husband and wife. You may kiss the bride," the pastor said, smiling at them.

Chad pulled her veil back over her head and leaned down, his arms going around her. His mouth descended on hers—a kiss of reverence, love, and joy.lu

"May I present Mr. and Mrs. Chad and Rachel McCarthy," the pastor announced.

Everyone stood, clapping and cheering, expressing their own joy in this special moment.

"Mrs. Rachel McCarthy. I like the sound of that," Chad whispered. He took her by the hand and led her down the aisle.

"I'm kind of partial to it myself," she teased. Her heart swelled with love for her husband. This wasn't anything she would have thought possible when she first returned home, but God had shown her anything was possible. It was something she would strive to remember in the coming years. *Faith.*

Chad beamed, equally showing how much this moment meant to him. "The first day of the rest of our lives, and I can't wait to dance with my new bride."

"For someone who didn't think he was much of a romantic, you sure do have a way with words," she said, laughing up at him as they made their way to the reception area.

"Between you and God, I never stood a chance."

The changes in Chad had been remarkable after he opened his heart to the Word and let himself get help for his own emotional well-being. Her new husband had a huge heart, and he wasn't afraid to share it with the world, and it showed in everything he did to help the kids who needed someone to guide and nurture them past their own pain and emotional hurts.

It wasn't long before the music started, and she was in her father's arms for the father-daughter dance. "You are the bride of the century," he said, pulling her close.

Resplendent in his tux, she was proud of him and the way he and her mother had banded together to help make the wedding a fast reality. "Thank you. But I'm your daughter; you have to say that." She grinned.

Her father shook his head. "The difference is, I mean it. You followed your own heart, taking control of your future. I'm proud of you, and I probably don't say it enough, but I love you."

Rachel brushed away the tears that fell. "I love you too, Daddy."

"I hope you don't mind, but your mother and I bought you a sizable wedding present. One we hope you will love, but if you don't, I promise you can exchange it for something you do like," he said, all without looking at his feet or missing a step. Her father had always been a fantastic dancer.

"I would never exchange or return anything you've picked out to give us, as it's a gift given with love."

He shook his head and grinned. "You don't know what it is yet, so I won't hold you to that."

"Fair enough. If it's some really ugly bowl I'll never use in this lifetime, I promise I'll exchange it and not tell you. Deal?" She was teasing. Ugly or otherwise, she would keep the gift.

"Deal," he said, leaning down to kiss her cheek as Chad approached.

"It's time for me to claim my bride in a dance," he said, reaching for Rachel's hand.

Her mother joined them on the dance floor. "Did you tell her?" she asked.

Rachel looked back and forth between her parents, wondering what they were up to.

"Sort of." He shrugged.

"Well then, Mr. Harrelson, get on with it so you can come dance with me." Her mother only had eyes for her father as she laid her hand on his arm.

"Anything you say, dear. I was only waiting for you to join us." Her father reached into his pocket and pulled out a gift box and handed it to Chad.

A quick glance in her direction, Chad was equally intrigued by what this would be. Of course, with her parents, there was no telling. But whatever the gift was, it certainly wasn't an ugly bowl.

Chad lifted the lid, and inside there was a key with a tag. He held it up for Rachel's inspection.

She read the tag and was more than a little confused. "The tag says welcome home. Please don't tell me it's a key to the house. I already have one, and Chad and I are not living with you when we get back from Alaska." She said she wouldn't return a gift, but this one fell into the category of not accepting. *Big difference.*

"No, dearest daughter of mine. I'm an empty nester and plan to stay that way. But the house at the end of the street went up for sale, and we bought it for you. As a wedding present. It will be nice for Sunday dinners and cookouts. And grandkids," her mother added. "Don't you think it's a wonderful idea?"

Rachel shook her head, trying to find her tongue and the right words. "A house. You gave us a house." Saying the words didn't help it sink in any easier. It was a generous gift but a controlling one.

"Yes, dear. You know the one. It's very nice. You've always admired it, and I thought it would be perfect. Was I right?" her mother asked, uncertainty lacing her voice.

Rachel knew the one. And her mother was right—it was perfect.

"Thank you so much. This is such an incredible gift," Chad said, hugging both her mother and father.

"You don't even know what house, Mr. McCarthy," Rachel teased.

"Anywhere you are, is okay by me, Mrs. McCarthy."

"Well, in that case, it is perfect. It's the dreamiest house, and we will have built-in babysitters," Rachel said, a gleam in her eye as she mentioned children. They hadn't discussed any timelines or plans other than to know they both wanted children. Lots of them.

Chad shook his head. "Just not right away. I want my wife to myself for a while." He chuckled.

"You're going away for six months. How much more time do you need?" her mother asked.

"All but a week of that, I must share her time with the other volunteers at the Outreach Center. Not nearly enough."

Leslie joined them. "Hey, everyone. The dance? You do remember why we are all here, don't you?" She pointed to the stage where everyone stood watching and waiting for the wedding dance.

Rachel blushed. "Yes, yes. But my parents just gave us a house for a wedding gift," she squeaked. Her dream house.

Leslie's mouth dropped open in surprise as she glanced at Chad for confirmation. "Nice, but I reckon my gift will pale in comparison."

"Anything from you will be treasured, dear sister. I promise."

"You never told him," Leslie asked.

Rachel shrugged, shaking her head but unable to keep from grinning. "Nope. Left it as a surprise. But on that same subject, I do have something important to tell you, Chad. We got our job assignments at the Outreach Center in Alaska."

"Please tell me we'll be on the construction team. Something rugged and manly, and working in the great outdoors," Chad said.

"Nope. The cooking team. A team of two providing all the meals to the volunteers," she said, the irony of the position not lost on anyone standing there.

Chad most of all. "No way. Did you tell them we can't cook?"

Maybe it was her fault, or perhaps it was fate, but it was a done deal. She'd already sent the acceptance response, knowing they'd agreed it didn't matter. "We were late on the list to sign up, so I checked the box '*anything.*' I mean, what were the odds?" she asked, still more than a little in shock over the situation.

"Apparently, too high. I reckon we'll be thrown out of Alaska and needing a home sooner than we thought. But, at least we will have the cabin as a retreat, and I can get my mountain time in that way." His easy attitude and ability to see the humorous side of things were two things she loved about him. But then there were so many.

"The good news is this assignment is only for six months," Rachel added.

"It sounds like my gift will be even more valuable than I thought," Leslie chimed in.

"So you really did it?" Rachel asked. Talk about true irony. She had told Leslie it would be a waste of time, but apparently, her friend had gone through with her original plan as a wedding present.

"I did." Leslie grinned, thrilled with her now and all-too-important gift.

"What is she talking about?" Chad asked.

"Cooking lessons. I thought Leslie was joking. Turns out I was wrong," Rachel said, smiling at her husband.

"You two's cooking is nothing to joke about. Yikes!" Leslie said, twisting away when Rachel sought to slap her arm. "I set you both up with online cooking classes. Sounds like you will have a hungry audience to practice on. Bon appétit, big brother."

"You rascal. Although, I've had Rachel's cooking, so nice job."

"Hey, I'm standing right here. And you're cooking is just as bad," Rachel retorted.

"That it is," Chad admitted.

"Mom and Dad, thank you, your gift is incredible." Rachel hugged her parents, and Chad seconded her words of gratitude.

Rachel hugged her friend. "And thank you, Leslie. Your gift may save the mission trip. At the very least, the volunteers will appreciate it."

"Now, may I have this dance?" Chad asked, pulling her into his arms.

"You may." Rachel let him lead her to the dance floor, and the two danced the waltz as one. Completely in time. Of course, there were lessons involved, but they were paying off. Just like the cooking lessons would pay off.

"Are you sure you're okay with going to Alaska for six months?" Rachel asked as other couples joined them on the floor.

Chad nodded. "I will compromise in life, but not in love."

It was the sweetest words she'd ever heard. "I love you, husband of mine."

"I love you too, sweetheart."

Together they would dance through life and love with God and their faith as a guide.

***

If you enjoyed this sweet and charming romance, be sure to check out the
ALSO BY ELSIE DAVIS section on the next page for more clean and wholesome romance.

BONUS READ

Want to keep in touch with new releases and what's happening in the world of Elsie Davis?
Sign up for the monthly newsletter at Elsie Davis HEA (Happily-Ever-After) and enjoy DIGGING THE DRIVER (A Celebrity Corgi Romance) as a FREE BOOK!

The greatest compliment you could give an author is to leave a review in order to help other readers discover the same great stories you enjoyed. Amazon/Bookbub/Goodreads are all great places. Many thanks!!!
Another great way to keep in touch - *Follow Elsie Davis on FaceBook*

Also By Elsie Davis

Sweet, Clean and Wholesome Stories...with a Happily-Ever-After Guarantee!

Holidays in Hallbrook

(Sweet Romance Series for Holidays Throughout the Year)

Welcome to Hallbrook, New Hampshire. A small-town filled with the unexpected, lots of love, and of course, a beloved dog to ramp up the excitement.

Love & Order (Labor Day)

Love & Family (Thanksgiving)

Love & Peace (Christmas)

Love & Chocolate (Valentine's Day)

Love & Hope (Mother's Day)

Love & Liberty (Independence Day)

Love & Honor (Veteran's Day)
Love & Joy (Easter)
Love & Adventure (Father's Day)

Great Smoky Mountain Getaways
(Christian Inspirational – Women's Fiction Romances)
Juliet's Journey to Love
Poppy's Path to Love
Rachel's Road to Love

Crossroads Creek Cowboys
(Christian Inspirational Romances)
The Heart of a Cowboy
The Help of a Cowboy
The Return of a Cowboy
Coming Soon – The Care of a Cowboy

Crestfield Inn Romances
If you like special kinds of soulmates, a splash of the supernatural, and wholesome relationships,

you'll adore this sweet bit of fun filled with ro-
mance and mystery.
Turning Back Time
Turning Up Roses
Turning Down Pie

Celebrity Corgi Romance
(Standalone Sweet Romance)
If you like light mystery mixed in with your hap-
pily-ever-after, you'll enjoy this second-chance
romance and the race to save an adorable Corgi.
Digging the Driver

Gold Coast Retrievers
(Sweet Romance)
*Special Golden Retrievers help their humans solve
mysteries, save lives, and even find love...*
Defending Dakota

Trinity River
(Sweet Western Romance)

Ranchers and farmers depend on the Trinity River for water, but when a secret conglomerate starts buying up property by fair means or foul, it's time for the landowners of Tumble County to fight back—Texas style. But what they don't count on, is finding love in the process.

Back in the Rancher's Arms

Small Town, Big Secrets

Coming Soon! (2023-2024)

Sundancer's Legacy – 9 Book series

Sundancer's Star

Sundancer's Joy

Sundancer's Heart

Sundancer's Majesty

Sundancer's Miracle

Sundancer's Glory

Sundancer's Kiss

Sundancer's Moon

Sundancer's Splendor

About The Author

Elsie Davis is a *USA Today and International Best-selling Author* of over 25 sweet, clean, and wholesome romances, and a member of the ACFW. She discovered the world of Happily-Ever-After romance at the age of twelve when she began avidly reading Barbara Cartland, the Queen of Romance, and has been hooked ever since. After building her dream log home on top of a small mountain, she turned her attention to do what she loves most, writing. Elsie writes sweet Contemporary Romance and Contemporary Christian Romance from her heart...hoping to share a little love in a big world.

When she's not writing, she can be found birding, kayaking, camping, fishing, playing disc golf, and taking nature walks—hoping to spot wildlife. Basically, she loves all things outdoors, EXCEPT cold weather. She and her husband are avid Caribbean cruisers, but Elsie's favorite vacation was their cruise to Alaska. (In spite of the cold!) Indoors, she enjoys a toasty fire, and of course, a great romance with a guaranteed Happily-Ever-After.

https://www.elsiedavishea.com

www.ingramcontent.com/pod-product-compliance
Lightning Source LLC
Chambersburg PA
CBHW021151310726
48971CB00002B/579